RILEY

JASPER SPRINGS

BOOK FIVE

BY EVIE RILEY

Riley

An MM Age Gap Romance

Jasper Springs

Book Five

Copyright © 2024

Evie Riley

Second Edition

ISBN: 978-1-77357-688-6

Published by Naughty Nights Press LLC

Cover Art By Willsin Rowe

RILEY

Secrets.

High expectations.

A truth revealed.

Riley Evans is counting down the days to his brother's wedding. If only he could find a date for the big day.

When a chance meeting during karaoke night finds Riley's plus one up for wager, Riley finds himself the winner in more ways than one.

Too bad his love game isn't as strong as his pool game.

A self-made OnlyFans man, Eric Olsen has built his entire life being the man everyone desires. Being Riley's date to the hottest wedding in Jasper Springs should be an easy win, but Eric soon finds himself desiring the sweet-as-pie art teacher.

If only he could come clean about his life and his feelings.

Will Riley break free from the chains of expectation? Or will Eric embrace his truth at the expense of losing the man he wants most?

Readers seeking an age gap romance with a little hint of D/s set in a cozy little town may find this story fills the bill. While Riley and Eric may have cameos in future stories, each book in this series can be read as a standalone.

CHAPTER ONE

Eric

I CHECKED MY watch for the second time in five minutes. The cafe was bustling at this hour and I couldn't help but wonder if he was here, somewhere, looking for me.

Though, to be fair, I looked a lot different with my clothes on.

Maybe I should start bringing pictures of my dick to these meet-ups so people can identify me better.

I sighed, taking a sip of my coffee as I watched folks hustle in and out of the cafe. A couple of nonchalant stares and whispers from some women told me they either thought I was cute or they recognized me from my work.

Despite my audience being made up of mostly men, I knew there were plenty of women out there who were into my performances, if only by the sheer amount of "I want to choke on this dick" and "fill me up Daddy" comments I received on my Daily Cum Shot threads from cock thirsty women subscribers.

I bounced my leg with anticipation, checking my watch again.

My blind date was now fifteen minutes late.

Or he wasn't coming at all.

I would bet it was the latter.

I wasn't ashamed of what I did for a living by any means. Though I'd learned to at least keep the "Hi, I'm Eric, you might know me from Only Fans as *XxPrinceAyricxX*" to myself until they at least showed up.

I could swipe right on anyone when it came to hooking up, but I wasn't looking for someone to just placate my sexual desires. If I wanted that, I could have anyone I wanted.

Call me crazy, but I wanted *more*. Sex might have been my job, and I wasn't lacking when it came to dick. What I was lacking though, was substance. I wanted someone to *love* me, and I'm not talking about the me that half a million people watched daily. I wanted someone who I could play video games and watch stupid gay movies with, but also someone who wouldn't bat an eye at eating sushi off my dick.

What can I say, I have priorities.

You'd think as a man who interacts with thirsty subscribers for a living, I would be more than fulfilled. But the truth was, every day I turned off my webcam, spent from my performance, and I felt empty as shit.

And the deafening silence of my townhome was not helping my mental health when everything screamed, "You are alone!"

Just once, I wanted to see someone else loafing on my couch, someone else raiding my fridge.

Someone else using my shampoo and shower gel.

I wanted to walk down the street with someone respectable, some modern-day prince charming with a cup of coffee, I wanted to wake up next to a man who wasn't going to leave after breakfast and never come back.

I drained the last bit of my coffee as my notifications went off on my phone one after the other.

No doubt the masses were all commenting their praise and dirty thoughts, as I'd only just posted my latest video an hour ago, right before I left for this blind date my friend, Julie, *insisted* I go on.

I found it easier to try and get to know a guy if I unloaded a round first. I wasn't one of those guys who could go multiple rounds when I was performing, despite my stamina training. Maybe when I was in college I could pull that off, but now, I needed a break in between, partially because it took a lot of focus and concentration—as well as training—to be able to perform at the level my subscribers required, and to get a good, full shot for the camera.

Which is why I only posted once a week now instead of the two or three times a week I posted when I started my OF.

I got up, headed to the trash to pitch my coffee as a text came in among the strings of OF notifications.

Buried beneath the "I want that all over me," and the "need someone to suck that?" comments, Julie's bright purple icon blinked at me.

I'm waiting...

I huffed a sigh as I texted her back.

Yeah, me too. Your mark never showed.

I casually strolled to my black Benz—the first big purchase I'd made after I switched from amateur camming to the big leagues and opened my OF. I'd worked my ass off—well, my cock off too—to have the things I did. My townhome, my car, my top of the line sneaker collection.

But once men heard *how* I'd made a living for myself—despite the fact my job actually consisted of more than just coming on camera every day—their damn balls disappeared and suddenly I became a damn leper, and most of them just never called me again.

Julie typed away.

What? Are you sure?

I rolled my eyes as the car unlocked, picking up on the signal from the keys in my pocket.

I arrived ten minutes early so I could get my coffee, and just left. I waited for a half hour, Jules. No one approached me.

I'd even worn my "nice" blazer, the purple velvet one that made me look sophisticated, yet stylish.

It was easy to pick out a bright purple jacket amidst the muted tones of Jasper Springs's average population, which was why I'd chosen it.

I started the car, feeling defeated.

You didn't tell him about the OF, did you?

I hoped Julie had remembered to keep her mouth shut. Lord knew, when she got to talking sometimes, shit just slipped out.

Of course I didn't. You asked me not to. She responded, quickly adding, *I told him you work in social media.*

That was the understatement of the year.

My shoulders fell as anxiety crept in.

It was a small town, what were the odds they looked me up?

That maybe they already knew?

Slim, probably, but not zero.

I was careful to keep my public profile separate from my OF, but if someone really wanted to dig around, I'm sure they could find out what my *self-owned business* was.

Oh well. Another one bites the dust, I guess.

Guess I'm just chopped liver then. I texted back.

I'm sorry, Eric. Maybe something happened, do you want me to reach out and ask?

I considered her words as I pulled out of the parking lot.

The last thing I wanted was to appear desperate, even to Julie. If some asshole couldn't be bothered to show up, why should I beg for his attention?

But a part of me wanted to believe that maybe there was a good reason. Maybe something came up at work, or maybe they had to rescue a fucking cat from a tree or some shit. Anything.

But I was already over the situation, and I wanted to move on. I wanted to forget about being overlooked yet again, because I didn't want to go down the road of self-loathing.

What I wanted to do was to get a drink and maybe find some hot piece of ass to take home and numb the pain of rejection for a little while.

Just for the night, anyway, since apparently that's all I was capable of landing.

No, it's fine. Don't worry about it, Jules. Thanks anyway.

I tossed the phone on the passenger seat, not even bothering to check her response as I sped toward M's Place.

CHAPTER TWO

Riley

I HATED FRIDAYS. For starters, every Friday was school spirit day, and no matter what the season, there was always a pep rally or a game, and catching up on the end of the week reports and tests while trying to balance curriculum planning for the following week was exhausting.

But today, I felt worse than normal because I'd fucked up entirely and forgot about the blind date Julie—my brother's fiancée's bridesmaid and a long-time friend of mine—had tried to set me up on.

EVIE RILEY

To be fair, I'd fully intended on showing up, but when my principal showed up five minutes before I was ready to head out with a stack of paperwork for me regarding my annual school art trip to DC in a few months, I knew I was done for.

My job always came first because my job, my students were my life.

Because I had no life of my own, not really. Sure, I hung out with my brother and his friends, my coworkers sometimes, but I wasn't anyone's first choice.

Because all my friends are either married or engaged.

I'd never had time for romance, and now, here I was an eternally single art teacher in his late thirties who couldn't even tell his boss *no* when I had a fucking date.

But I wasn't fast enough, because my blind date—who was supposed to be wearing a purple blazer—was nowhere to be found in the otherwise dead cafe, when I'd arrived. I needed a drink, and in this town there really was only one watering hole to go to that was openly queer friendly and actually had decent drinks.

M's Place was packed, as always. Normally, I despised crowds in tiny spaces, and M's Place was definitely a small space. Maxine somehow managed to squeeze a postage stamp size stage in between the bar and an alcove that was some hodge-podge mashup of pool, arcade games, and one of those weird antique Love Magnet Meter games from the fifties in between the thirty high top tables and ten booths, while making the place open and friendly and not claustrophobic. Which was a damn miracle.

It was probably fate that I'd run into my brother and his wedding party at the bar. Though knowing Giselle, she was fixing to make this a weekly shindig.

I sipped my beer as Julie nudged me.

"What happened with your blind date earlier?" she asked.

I sighed, running a hand through my hair. "I got held up at work, actually. Principal Weatherly dropped off a shit ton of papers regarding the trip and—"

"Shit, you missed it?" she asked, biting her lip.

"I mean, I went, but... he was gone.

Can't say I blame him, you know. I was like, forty minutes late."

Julie pursed her lips. I shrugged in defeat.

Just as I opened my mouth, I saw Grayson—my future in-law—and his new boyfriend, Henry—Giselle's friend and bridesmaid Mia's brother—strolling into the bar arm in arm like they owned the damn place.

We'd all spent last weekend together in the mountains, but both Grayson and Henry didn't seem too keen on socializing with me. Well, I guess technically, looking back on the weekend, it made sense now, but at the time it felt like I just wasn't cool enough to join their little club.

To be honest, I'd always been like that. An outsider. My brother was always the popular one, and I was just the social outcast who preferred history books to keggers in the woods.

That's why I'd brought Cadence, my TA, with me to the weekend trip.

My brother, Aaron, and I got along just fine as long as the topic was sports related, or involved some sort of competition. Which wasn't hard when I worked for our alma mater, Jasper Springs High. Our football team, the Jasper Springs Otters had gone undefeated last year.

But I needed more than just someone to casually grunt and chime in.

Not to mention Aaron was the star quarterback when we were in high school, which was what?

Damn near twenty years ago now?

I smiled as Grayson and Henry arrived at our table and everyone made introductions. Julie excused herself to go to the ladies room, Giselle and Mia hot on her heels.

Henry's grin was enviable, and Grayson's natural air exuded a confidence that was also quite admirable.

I was genuinely happy they seemed to be happy, just like everyone else in Giselle and Aaron's party, but I still felt a sting of jealousy being the only single guy in the party.

"Where's Cadence?" Aaron asked, pulling me from my thoughts.

"Probably having a better night than me," I said, wanting to avoid the question I knew was coming.

"She your plus one?"

"No," I said flatly, then taking a long drink.

"Why not? She seems nice. Not to mention she's got a killer rack," Aaron teased, nudging me. "Mom and Dad would love her..." he said with a laugh.

I rolled my eyes. He wasn't wrong, but he also knew pussy didn't do it for me.

My family always assumed I'd settle down, especially being in the line of work I was. Of course, I wanted to settle down too, but I didn't have the heart to tell my parents it wasn't with a woman. My brother understood the fact that I was as gay as a hot pink toaster, and he always told me I was being dramatic. That it wouldn't matter who I was with, that they wouldn't care as long as I was happy. But that was easy for someone like my brother to say. He was getting married to the daughter of one of the most well known families in Jasper Springs. Giselle was practically Miss Americana.

Aaron was more than supportive though. Hell, he even tried to hook me up with a gay or bi friend once or twice. But those guys, they didn't want relationships. They wanted to fuck around, and while that had been fun in my college years, as a thirty-eight year old high school art teacher, I needed something more than just a guy with good deep-throating skills.

Who am I kidding?

Hell, I probably need that too, since my sex life is about as dry as the Sahara these days.

"Mom and Dad would love any woman I brought to the wedding, even if she was a lesbian."

Aaron laughed, shaking his head. "True. You have a point. But at this rate, you're going to have to hire a date for the wedding," he said with a laugh.

I rolled my eyes again. "You sound like my coworkers," I grumbled.

While my parents had not yet given up on the dream I'd meet the right woman, my coworkers were practically sending me singles profiles for men within a thirty mile radius or trying to set me up on blind dates every chance they got.

Just earlier in the school day I'd gotten into a debate with my classroom neighbor, Chris, about literally *hiring* an escort like my life was a LGBTQ version of the Wedding Date or something.

"I'm just saying, the deadline fast approaches... and no one wants to be alone at a wedding," he said.

"I'm not *alone*. I'm the best man."

"You don't technically have a partner."

"And even if I did find a date in time for your wedding, it's not like they'll be up there with me," I reminded him. "For God's sake, I'm a glorified ring bearer."

My brother sighed, obviously deciding this conversation was a lost cause, switching gears, instead challenging Grayson and Henry to a pool match.

I sighed, my shoulders sinking. Perhaps I just needed a distraction. Something to take my mind off my impending singleness. Something to relieve some stress.

So I agreed to play with the boys, if only for a little while. It was a school night, after all.

"You guys wanna play?" Aaron asked the group of guys who were *sitting* all over the pool tables lazily enjoying their beers.

They were a small group of three, two

of them some twenty-somethings who looked more 'bro' than man, with their hats on backward, their perfectly trim beards, and their flannels too tight fitting.

"Sure," the one in the front said, setting down his beer. The only one without a hat who looked older than twenty-one, brushed his hand through his dark hair, pushing up off the table with ease. While his friends sported the same buffalo plaid flannel, their unphased sexy leader sported a black fitted tee shirt that showed off his rather toned arms. His striking blue eyes glittered underneath the low light of the bar, and I couldn't help but think he was *hot.*

The kind of hot you dream about because you know you'll never have a chance of landing someone *that* sexy.

"Eric, you're on my team," bro number one nipped at Mr. Blue Eyes.

"Name's Aaron, this here is my brother, Riley, and that's my future brother in law, Grayson, and his boyfriend, Henry."

Mr. Blue Eyes smirked, grabbing his beer.

"Pleasure to meet you, boys," he said with a grin. "I'm Eric, these here assholes are my associates, Jordan and Sticky."

I furrowed my eyebrows. "What kind of a name is Sticky?" I asked in disgust. The man known as *Sticky* came forward, laughing darkly.

"My name is actually *Stanley, handsome,* but my subs call me Sticky," he said with a gaze that was more predatory than anything I'd ever seen. It made me uncomfortable.

"Yeah, cause you don't know how to keep your fucking hands to yourself," Eric snapped, and Sticky scoffed.

"You ain't never complained," Sticky retorted.

Eric passed me a pool cue and some chalk. "Don't mind him, he was dropped on his head as a small child. It's the brain damage," he said.

I took the polished stick from his hands, my fingers grazing his. "Noted," I said, relishing in the warmth, the smoothness of his touch.

"You suckers ready to lose?" Jordan taunted.

Eric smiled wickedly.

"How about we make this a little more interesting?" my brother said, as Jordan, Sticky, and Eric took their places.

"How so?" Jordan asked, nodding at us.

"Loser buys the winner a round of drinks," Aaron suggested.

Grayson squared his shoulders as he set the balls.

Eric smirked, his gaze roving over me.

"Famous last words, boys. Let's play."

CHAPTER THREE

Eric

ONE GAME TURNED into two games, and because I'm a man of my word, I bought the new guys a round of drinks.

I had to admit, Aaron, Grayson, Henry, and Riley were all pretty good opponents, and it was nice to have a challenge for once.

Riley shifted his weight as he turned to me for a moment.

"So..." he started, and a part of me felt bad for the guy.

I could tell he wanted to talk, probably even flirt a little, but his Sunday School get up of a green polo and khakis and messy bronze hair was surprisingly not as much of a turnoff as it should have been.

Maybe I'm just all messed up because of earlier. Maybe I just need to fuck myself right again.

"If you ask me about the weather or sports, I will throw this beer in your face," I taunted him.

Riley blinked, his mouth agape. "Well, what would you advise I ask you about, Eric?" he said, crossing his arms, the pool stick held between his toned arms, making me think of other things. "Got any pointers on losing?" he taunted.

What are you like, five, dude?

I scoffed at his juvenile insult, though I couldn't deny it stirred a need to show this man exactly how to take a loss.

On his knees with my cock stuffed down his throat.

I shifted, if only to try and dispel the rowdy serpent in my pants.

"How about you ask what you really want, Riley?" I said, batting my lashes at him, my tongue sarcastic as hell.

Where did that come from?

Riley scoffed, shaking his head. "Forget it," he said.

It was Jordan's turn in our second game, when the girls arrived.

"Hey you..." I said when I realized Julie came with the group.

Julie's mouth fell open in surprise, as she glanced between Riley and I, our backs against the wall, separated by none other than an old-timey love machine game.

Seriously, who played those things anymore?

I thought they wiped them all off the face of the earth.

"Well, fancy meeting you here, Eric," Julie said, pulling my attention away from the tall, blushing man beside me.

I leaned in to hug her, catching a whiff of her perfume and nearly choking on it.

She pulled away with a grin. "I thought you'd be home nursing your wounds," she teased.

"You two know each other?" Riley asked, fidgeting with his stick again, running his hands up and down the length in repeated motion.

Instinctively, my body and brain jumped to sexy thoughts about what his stick actually looked like, and what a show it would be to watch him.

Sprawled out all over my bed, hand wrapped around his cock.

Riley was tall. I'd probably peg him at six two, but he carried himself with stature. My mama always said God let things grow until they were perfect, and at a nice old five foot nine, I supposed Sky Daddy knew to quit while he was ahead.

I might have been on the shorter side compared to most, but my cock made up what I lacked in height easily.

Still, I knew big dudes came with big sticks, and I was a size queen.

Plus, I was still peeved after I'd been stood up by my blind date.

"Eric, you're up," Jordan said, drowning his beer as he flashed his gaze at Julie.

"Why, hello..."

"Leave her alone, Jordy. She's taken," I said, flashing a wink.

Julie laughed as I lined up my shot, retorting some burn at Jordan that made the rest of the guys holler and Jordan curse.

Setting my gaze on my prize, I couldn't help but notice Riley in my field of vision. Or more accurately, Riley holding his stick in front of him, front and center to his dick, distracting me for the moment.

My own cock twitched as I licked my lips, trying to focus on the balls in front of me instead of the ones out of reach.

I'd been swiping right on matches for the last two years. On top of the fact I regularly shared my most intimate moments with half a million subscribers, I had a keen sense of gaydar.

In a nutshell, I knew when someone wanted to fuck me. At this point, it was like a sixth sense or something.

And the way Riley kept staring at me, it was more than obvious. Not to mention his conversation skills.

I would have bet the farm that he hadn't had a good lay in while.

Something about that realization made me feel both guilty and intrigued.

My phone buzzed in my pants pocket, no doubt my comments going off still. They'd be going off all night.

Until I posted my next video, to appease my thirsty masses.

I took my shot, watching as the balls dispersed, clacking against each other as they came together. The eight ball slowly rolled, knocking another ball into the corner pocket, causing me to curse.

"Damn it!" I said, pressing my lips together. I'd been too distracted by khaki-covered groins and the ever present buzzing of my phone against my ass to make a proper shot.

I totally missed.

"Nice try," Riley said tauntingly as he pushed off the wall, smirking at me. "Maybe you should aim for the ball you want to hit."

The sight of his lips turning up in the corner, the way he cockily squared his shoulders as he sauntered to where I stood was a damn rush. Heat enveloped me as he nudged me aside with his hip.

How fucking dare he!

"Now, let me school you in how it's really done," he teased, positioning himself to take his shot.

I ran a hand through my sweaty hair. If he made this shot, that would be twice we'd lost. And I certainly didn't want to lose. Anger flooded me as well as a fresh current of desire, because his words only made me want to put him in his place.

Bent over the fucking pool table.

I hate losing.

I took a pull of my beer as Julie settled beside me, crossing her arms. Sticky settled on the other side of me, and we watched long-limbed Riley angle himself, bending over the table. His arms were long, toned and trim and drew attention to his fingers. I watched as he curled his hand around the base of his stick, which was not helping the current erection in my pants or my competitive fantasy about teaching him how to fucking aim for the bullseye.

I shifted my weight as I focused on my drink.

"See something you like?" Julie teased.

"I'm not sure yet," I said honestly.

Sticky nudged me. "What's there to consider? The guy's been staring at you all night."

"Yeah, well, staring is creepy," I nipped at Sticky. I wasn't sure why I felt so on the spot, so vulnerable. Maybe it had to do with the beers I was pounding back. I'd lost track after the third...

Sticky and Jordan were the closest things I had to brothers. I'd met them at an adult entertainers expo a while back, shocked to hell and back that they were both Jasper Springs natives like me.

In this town of bake sales and cookie-cutter families, it was nice to have people who weren't judgmental of what I did for living.

Because they were doing the same thing. Having friends who understood the ins and outs of the business, the work that actually went into being the object of so many people's desires, made my job feel a lot less lonely.

Except Sticky and Jordan were more than just friends. They were a package deal. They both were on the platform too, producing similar content to mine, except they did it together.

More like they did each other.

For the fans, of course, despite the fact neither of them were gay.

Sticky was... well, Sticky. I didn't think he had a preference for anyone as long as they had a hole and were willing to put up with his stupidity. We'd fucked around a few times over the years, but I always felt like shit afterward, which is why we'd stopped.

Jordan was as straight as Riley's pool stick. Or at least, he *insisted* he was. My guess was he was probably bi and he just hadn't come to terms with it yet.

They were both also eternal bachelors, like me.

Who happened to live together, and who happened to fuck once in a while...

Christ, even Sticky has someone to share shit with, even if he's just a fucking coworker who's not as straight as he thinks.

"Hey, Riley," Julie called.

Riley turned to look at us briefly. "Yeah?"

"Wanna sweeten the deal?" she asked.

Aaron, Grayson, and Henry turned to face us, Jordan looking up from his beer.

Oh no, this can't be good. I know that look..."

"How so?" Jordan asked skeptically.

Julie shrugged as she set her gaze on Riley.

"Uh..." Riley raised an eyebrow.

Julie smirked, turning to Jordan. "Well, you see Aaron over there is getting married... and Riley here needs a plus one..."

Aaron laughed, fist bumping the air.

"Yes! I'm so in!"

"What?" Riley's face paled. "Jules... No..."

"If Riley scores this shot, *Eric* will have to accompany him," she said, practically grinning from ear to ear.

Well, isn't that interesting.

Julie cast me a wicked gin.

"And if we win..." Jordan grinned in return. "Loser has to pose for the Jasper Springs Hotties Calendar." Jordan grinned. "Which I happen to, uh... do some work for.".

He was the calendar's number one model, next to that local firefighter who thought he was the next Brad Pitt. Dawson something or other...

"We'll do it!" Aaron and Sticky called out in unison.

Fuck.

I wasn't opposed to being someone's plus one, and I'd be lying if I said I'd never been auctioned off before—that was for a charity event Jordan had gotten roped into—but the idea of accompanying Cinderella to the ball made my insides heat like an inferno.

Yeah, it's probably the beer.

Riley shook his head, dispelling the

hoots and barks, leaning closer, sliding his pool stick in between his fingers. Back and forth, back and...

"Fuck!" I said as I was literally smacked in the groin by the end of Riley's stick, my hardness now ebbing with pain as my balls stung.

Immediately, I covered my aching junk, knocking over the remainder of my beer and spilling it all over Julie.

"Oh my God!" Julie cried as Aaron and Co. screamed, "We won!" over and over.

"Fucking ay!" I howled, sucking in a breath as Riley turned, his eyes wide in terror.

"I'm so sorry, Eric. I—"

"Fuck you," I snarled as I attempted to breathe.

Julie laughed as she shook off the spill.

"I think that's enough for one night," Aaron said with a grin. "It's been fun guys, but I think our work here is done," he said.

"Aw, fuck..." Jordan said, grabbing his coat.

"What?" Sticky asked.

"We've got an hour left until—"

Neither of them had to say anything, since I knew what time they usually posted. While I was a once a day guy, my friends posted multiple times in a day.

Sticky pulled the keys from his pocket, sliding his hand around Jordan's waist, nodding to me.

"You good, bro?" he asked.

Finally able to breathe, I nodded. "Peachy," I bit out as the crowd started to disperse.

"Do you, uh... need a ride?" Riley asked cautiously.

"That depends, Riley Rabbit," I huffed. "As long as you don't have any stray sticks laying around to whack me with—"

"I'm so sorry, the stick just... slipped."

I flashed my gaze up at him, conflicted by both the steamy thoughts and the reality at hand.

Yeah, I bet it slipped.

Cheater.

"Looks like you have a date for the wedding, after all," Julie said with a wink.

Riley blushed, like a damn Sunday School teacher as he ran his hand through his hair.

Fuck, she was right.

Now I had to honor my word.

I grumbled as I flipped her off, and she just laughed, leaving Riley and I in her dust.

"I'm so sorry, Eric, I— Let me make it up to you," he said as I grabbed my purple blazer from the back of my chair.

"Fine," I said, tossing it over my shoulder. "Let's get out of here."

CHAPTER FOUR

Riley

MY HEART WAS racing as we walked to the car.

For starters, Eric was hot. The guy was most certainly above my grade level when it came to the dating pool. Plus, judging by his bold fashion sense and his flawless skin, I'd garner he was in his late twenties, which meant he was at least a good ten years my junior.

While he'd agreed to the terms of winning and losing—being my *date*—he didn't seem all that into it.

Or me.

And then on top of everything, I damn

smacked the man in the balls—by accident, I swear—and now was trying to make up for my eternal fuck ups by at least giving him a ride home.

Maybe I'm just not cut out for dating in 2024.

I sighed in defeat, hoping that perhaps we could put this bullshit behind us, and maybe I could just tell him not to worry about the wedding.

I'd come up with some line or excuse for Aaron, and we could both just forget this whole thing ever happened.

I opened the passenger door to my blue sedan before he could do so himself.

I am, if anything, a gentleman, plus I did feel bad about hitting him in the balls earlier.

Eric's blue eyes sparkled in the parking lot light, surprised by the gesture.

"Thanks," he said, visibly swallowing.

"It's the least I can do," I said, waiting for him to take a seat before closing the door.

"Right," he said.

Within seconds, I was in the driver's seat, turning the car on without thinking.

The audiobook I'd had queued up prior to arrival blared through the speakers, which wouldn't have been a bad thing if it wasn't a damn *sex scene.*

Oh my God!

I tried to turn the app off on my phone, but it wouldn't budge.

"Shit!" I said as I fumbled for the right button to turn it off through the car speakers.

I took him into the back of my throat in one fell swoop until I couldn't breathe, his deep groan only making my own cock throb even more as he grabbed me by the back of my hair... "You take this cock so good, baby... just like Daddy likes it."

"I'm so sorry about this," I said, as I bashed my fingers against the display, trying to stop the most embarrassing moment of my life.

Yeah, there's no way this guy would go anywhere with me now.

Probably thinks I'm an absolute perv.

Fuck. My. Life.

Eric smirked devilishly as I finally managed to get the damn button to work and stop the dirty words from tumbling through my speakers. I looked at him, legs crossed with his velvet jacket in his lap, his head in his hands, thumb pressed to his mouth. He looked... amused.

"You seem to be doing a lot of apologizing tonight, Riley," he said, his voice dark and gravelly. "Your grievances are stacking up."

I couldn't help but turn scarlet at his tone, his words. "I know, I just..."

"Didn't think you were the audio porn type," he said with a raised eyebrow as I tapped my maps on the display.

"I'm not, it's not... it's not porn, it's literature," I defended.

Eric laughed. "Funny, historians say the same thing about the Marquis De Sade," Eric shrugged.

"Your address," I said bluntly, trying to steer the conversation away from where it was headed. Eric looked piqued, his grin deliciously provocative and his gaze intrigued. But I wasn't about to let a poignantly voiced sex scene carry us all the way home.

For starters, as I sat with my foot poised above the gas, I was acutely aware of all the blood rushing to my swollen cock, and the sight of Eric in my car, looking like sex on a stick combined with the lusty tones of my latest M/M smutty read, would be enough to crucify me forever.

I'd never live this night down in my own mind if I came in my pants like a damn teenager.

I was thirty-eight years old, for God's sake. Surely I could keep my dick in line for what, thirty minutes?

Eric shifted in his seat, his eyes dark with mischief. "You didn't say please," he touted.

I let out a choked laugh, swallowing my pride and my embarrassment as I implored him with my gaze.

"Please, Eric," I said softly, my pulse racing.

"Well, since you asked so nicely, and you are so keen on making up to me," he said as he leaned forward, tapping against the letters on the display, never looking at me once.

"But you should know for future reference, the correct answer is, 'Yes, *Daddy*.'."

My cock *throbbed* at his tone, his words, my mortification heating my body like a boiling pot.

Wait a minute... Was he... was he flirting with me?

"F... future reference?" I asked as he hit the green 'go' button, a sly grin on his face.

I threw the car into drive as he sat back languidly.

"Well, I am a man of my word, Riley, and the deal was I will accompany you to your little firehall wedding."

I scoffed at the idea of anyone calling Giselle's taste mediocre, or insinuating her wedding at the damn Paradise would be anything but black tie, or little in any manner. But then again, Eric had no idea Aaron was engaged to the Blake Lively of Jasper Springs, and how could he? He'd gone to the bathroom when Giselle kissed Aaron goodbye, heading home with Mia.

Not to mention, I didn't even know if Eric was a Jasper Springs resident, since I'd never seen him before, and as a teacher in this town, I knew almost *everyone.*

"You don't... you don't really *have to,* you know," I said with a sigh.

Though the idea of showing up with Eric on my arm *anywhere* made my entire body stiffen.

He was absolutely gorgeous, and I had a feeling he'd look impeccable in a nice suit, with a tie...

Images pushed forth in my mind of him standing above me, cufflinks shimmering in the light as he gazed down at me, running his hand over his...

No!

Don't go down that road!

Not now!

I glanced at the address on the maps app, if only to bring myself back to the here and now, surprised to notice it was indeed within Jasper Springs. In fact, it was part of Jasper Springs Estates, which I knew was the higher priced condos that housed some of Jasper Springs's upper crust.

I was pretty damn sure CEO Weston Rhodes and that town celeb, Drew Axel, just moved there, if I'm not mistaken.

The place had been a hot commodity lately.

"Will there be cake?" Eric asked, with a slight laugh.

"I mean, what wedding doesn't have a cake?" I retorted.

"Will there be alcohol?" he continued.

"I mean, probably top of the line considering it's Giselle..."

"Will you be all cleaned up and pretty in a nice fucking suit?" he asked, and I felt flushed, nervous.

All cleaned up and pretty...

Did he think... wait...

"Yes..." I squeaked.

"Well then, sounds like it'll be quite a night, don't you think?"

I laughed nervously. "I, uh... guess so?"

I passed the sign that read *Jasper Springs Estates,* lit up by the small spotlights. In the darkness, it looked almost ominous.

I cruised down the road, looking for his address number, focusing on anything but him.

"There," he pointed to a sleek, gray condominium. The spotlights in the yard cast shadows on it, illuminating it vividly.

The car rolled to a stop, and I turned it off, opening my door as Eric moved to open his.

When I came around to his side, he was just shutting the door. He fell back against the car for a moment, his gaze flashing up at me.

"What the fuck are you doing?" he asked, but his voice wasn't angry. It was curious. He didn't move. Instead, he just looked at me in question.

"Walking you to your door, obviously," I said, shaking my head.

"You don't have to do that," Eric said, shifting his weight, holding his jacket in front of him like a barrier.

I leaned against the car, biting my lip as I looked back at him. There was something about him that called to my inner gentleman. His apprehension at my polite conversation, at my opening of the car door.

I wondered about the partners in his life who hadn't shown him such etiquette.

That was another reason I despised trying to date in this day and age. Most men were the epitome of *I can do it myself.* I'd been told as much before, which made me feel quite ancient, despite the fact I wasn't even forty yet.

"I know, but..." I swallowed nervously as I offered him my arm. "Humor me?"

He looked at my arm like I'd grown three heads, and for a moment I didn't think he'd take it. But when his hand grasped my arm, just the slightest, I couldn't help but grin as I pulled him away from the car, slowly guiding us up his sidewalk, the air crisp against my skin.

It wasn't a long walk by any means, and we were on his porch within seconds. Eric dropped his hand, sliding it into his pockets for his keys.

I stood politely, waiting to watch him enter the door before I bounded back to my car, but he stood there for a moment in silence before he spoke.

"When's the last time you had fun, Riley?" he said, furrowing his eyebrows, forcing me to look at him in question.

"I beg your pardon?" I asked, confused by his question. It wasn't what I had expected.

"And I don't mean the kind of fun that ends with you home before midnight," he said, clearing his throat. "I'm talking about real honest to God, *fun.*" His voice came out dark and inviting, sending a chill snaking down my spine.

I wondered momentarily if his definition of fun differed from mine, almost sure that it did.

I paused, considering his question. I'd gone on the trip to Brideshead recently, but it wasn't what I'd call fun. I'd enjoyed myself, sure, as anyone in the beautiful expanse of nature with copious amounts of alcohol would. But I wasn't into drinking like the rest of my party mates, nor was I into watching everyone drunkenly make out.

I thought about the trips I took with my TA and my students every year. Last year we'd gone to Italy, and while I most certainly enjoyed myself, it was still awkward, at times. Mostly because I was the only single adult gay man on vacay, and engaging in any sort of romantic liaisons—or one night stands—was out of the question. My focus was on keeping my kids safe.

And sharing a room with my bestie slash coworker while also responsible for one hundred teenagers in a foreign country is not something I would call *fun* either. Not to mention, most of my free time during the year, and even in the summer, was devoted to volunteering for school events, programs, and curriculum.

I twisted my hands together, feeling the sweat overtake me. I wiped them on my pants, if only because the sudden heat as Eric stared at me was making me feel on display. I closed my eyes, and I sighed.

I could have told him anything, but instead I settled on the truth.

"It's been a while, I guess," I said.

Eric shifted.

"A while, huh?" he asked as he nodded at me, moving closer.

I looked down at the sliver of space between us. A part of me wanted to move closer, meet him halfway. To reach out and run my hands through his hair, and let myself have a little bit of *fun*.

To tease, to touch.

But I barely knew Eric, and I certainly didn't want to come off as one of those assholes who just took things without asking.

Eric clicked his tongue for a moment, before speaking. From this angle, I could feel the heat of his breath on my neck, the scent of whiskey and beer prevalent from his drinks earlier.

"Give me your phone," he commanded.

Every bone in my body, including the unruly one throbbing against my briefs stood at attention.

Because it wasn't what he said, it was *how* he said it.

With authority, with demand. It was the sexiest tone I'd ever heard a man use, and it made me want to drop to my knees on his fucking porch.

Maybe the smutty audiobooks were warping my brain.

Wordlessly, I drew my phone from my pocket, handing it to him. My hands were sweaty as he pulled it from me, his fingers grazing over my knuckles, sending fresh jolts of electricity racing through my veins.

I watched the light fall on his face, my heart in my throat. He tapped away furiously before handing me back my phone with a stoic gaze. I had a good amount of height on him, and I couldn't deny that the way he looked *up* at me, his tongue darting out to lick his lips, his bright blue eyes sparkling with mischief, made me feel as if I could melt into a puddle on his porch.

"Well, if we're going to do this, we should probably have a little fun with it.

So, next time you want to stay out past your bedtime, Cinderella, give me a call," he said as he turned around, inserted his keys in the lock, and then left me standing there, hard and wanting in a state of blissful confusion as I stared at his number on my phone. Conveniently written in as *Eric Olsen* with a legit eggplant emoji.

What was the eggplant supposed to symbolize again?

CHAPTER FIVE

Riley

"YOU DEFINITELY NEED to call him," Chris said, swiveling in my chair with his venti cold brew clutched in his fist. The scent of bitter coffee filled the room.

I stared at my phone on my desk in front of him, my arms crossed. "Yeah, but... what do I say?" I asked, my eyebrows furrowing.

Chris rolled his eyes. "You are hopeless, Riley, you know that right?" he said, bouncing his foot against his knee.

Glancing at the clock, I noted we had about fifteen minutes left for our lunch period. Fifteen minutes before a slew of seniors would traipse into my studio and destroy everything.

I swear high school kids are messier than the kindergartners.

"Tell me something I don't know," I huffed.

"Just ask him out for coffee or something. Surely you are capable of that, and if not, well, I can't help you there."

I nibbled at my fingernail, considering his words. Surely I could *text* a man to meet for coffee. It wasn't like I was asking him to marry me or something.

So why was I so fucking nervous?

"Yeah, coffee sounds good," I said, swallowing nervously.

Chris smirked at me. "You got a little crush, don't you?" he said with a laugh.

"I mean, yeah, I guess. He's attractive and..." I could feel myself heat as the memory of his dark voice, his bright blue eyes, pushed forth. "He's young," I settled on that word, whispering it into existence.

Chris's eyebrows furrowed. "How young?"

"Well, old enough to drink, for starters, but probably too young to know what a payphone is."

Chris laughed, shaking his head. "And he's got his own place in Jasper Springs Estates?" Chris whistled. "What is the guy a drug lord or something?"

It was my turn to roll my eyes. "God, I hope not," I said with a laugh.

"Maybe he's a high class escort," he said, wiggling his eyebrows.

"Or a mafia kingpin," I suggested with a laugh.

Chris shrugged. "Or a CEO of a Fortune 500 company who secretly owns a publishing company and a helicopter."

"He's not Christian Gray, Chris."

"You don't know that," he said as the bell rang. "All right, well, this has been fun but duty calls," he said as he pushed himself out of my chair.

The sounds of chattering teens filled the hallways, and I sighed, grabbing my phone and sliding it in my pocket.

"Keep me posted, Evans!" he said as he hit the doorframe with his palm on the way out.

"Yeah, yeah," I said with a wave, as students started to pour in.

CHAPTER SIX

Eric

"FIFTEEN MINUTES TO show time," I say to myself as I set my timer.

I hadn't slept the best the night before, and felt like I'd been dragging ass all day because of it.

But I guess Cinderella wasn't the only one who turned into a pumpkin after midnight.

I set about to setting my scene, making sure everything in my bedroom was clean. No photos on the nightstands, the covers freshly made and the pillows set just right.

I even made sure the floor was clear

of any and all dust, and then I went about setting the lights by using an app on my phone. I didn't film in my room often, but like I said, I was dragging ass.

Plus my AC unit in the studio was on the fritz again, which meant until I got a replacement part installed, I'd be filming in my room since it had good lighting, and of course, a bed.

I crawled onto my bed, leaning back against the pillows for a moment, in nothing but my black boxer briefs. A quick glance at my phone told me I had ten minutes till I went live. Which was just enough time for me to get comfortable.

I closed my eyes, letting my mind wander in my daily prep ritual as I slid my hand over my soft cock, pulling and tugging as I controlled my breath.

I had a myriad of fantasies that usually did the trick, and I tried to keep my prep fantasies on a rotating basis.

Today, it was a tall, sexy man in glasses, wearing khakis and a button down, staring down at me, telling me the only way to pass his class was if I did some extra credit.

I'd had this fantasy since college,

when I developed a crush on my Art History teacher.

He was straight though, so that extra credit would have landed me in the Dean's office, no doubt.

But a man *could* dream, right?"

I rubbed my chub through my briefs as the fantasy took hold. My viewers liked to be teased before the big reveal, and I noticed if I showed up with a visible tent first, prolonged the reveal a little, I got more likes and comments, which pushed the algorithm more.

Plus, I knew all my good angles.

I imagined Professor Hot Ass smacking his hand with a pointer stick, telling me if I didn't *beg* on my knees, he was going to strike me.

And then the strangest thing happened; Professor Hot Ass shifted in appearance.

In his place was Riley, the man who'd beat me at pool and nearly put an end to my moneymaker last night.

Who apparently had a thing for kinky audiobooks and needed a date to the school dance.

I mean... wedding.

But he did have that khaki wearing,

studio professor vibe to him that I was totally into.

And he was kind of cute, if I was being honest. All flustered over the dirty words, all sincere and walking me to my door and shit.

His dark eyes filled my psyche, causing my cock to twitch, just as the alarm went off.

I let go of myself, opening my eyes as I glanced around the room, almost as if I expected to find him there, watching.

I shook off the weird thoughts as I watched my computer load, waiting for the green light. Soon enough, I was live.

I waited momentarily for at least a few people to jump on before I addressed them.

I lowered my voice, rising to my knees as I made a show of lifting my cock, which was still quite hard and wanting.

Hearts bloomed across the screen as I leaned my head back, running my hand along my clothed shaft.

I carded my right hand through my hair as I used my left to continue stroking my cock. Turning to the side, I hunched over just enough to give a good side profile, enough to show the length and curve of my trapped cock, giving a good thrust to tease and titillate the viewers.

The tips came in quickly and I flashed them all a megawatt smile.

"I know what you guys really want," I said as someone commented, "Yes, Daddy, give it to me."

My mind decided that was the time to replay the smutty audio I'd heard in Riley's car, his blush filling his cheeks as he tried to shut it down.

You take this cock so good, baby... just like Daddy likes it.

My own cock throbbed at the word replay in my brain, and I had to suck in a breath.

"Take it off!" another commenter said as several more tips came in.

I sat back on my heels, sliding my underwear down just enough that my cock sprang free. I slid my hand back around my shaft, feeling its thickness and veins. I was *aching.*

And I was already sticky with precum.

What the hell?

I had masturbation down to a science. It was my job, after all. Usually,

I opened up with a nice tease in my pants, let the cock bob free, maybe smack it around a bit before I started to go to town.

I didn't want to waste a minute though, being as my subscribers were paying for entertainment and not my own existential crisis.

So, I pushed through.

I spit directly onto my cock, covering my shaft in saliva and gathering the precum from the head, slathering it down my hardness. I closed my eyes and my head fell back as I built my rhythm, the *ding ding* of comments and tips like a melodic overture of chimes.

"You take this cock so good, baby," I groaned, a fresh sheen of sweat blanketing my skin as I fucked my slick hand.

I let my free hand wander, pinching my nipples, sliding it down to my navel.

Chime, chime, chime.

The sound of success.

Images flashed in my mind of Riley on my porch, looking at me with big old puppy dog eyes.

I let my mind wander further, imagining him falling to his knees on my porch, those big, beautiful eyes wide with lust as I pulled out my thick cock.

"Just like Daddy likes it," I groaned, my voice all gravelly and dark.

Chime, chime, chime. Ding, ding, ding.

My cock swelled, throbbing with need as the sounds of my wet palm slapping against my dick echoed in the air. I fell forward on my knees, my underwear sliding down a bit to reveal half of my ass. I glanced up at my screen, making eye contact with my subs as I rocked my hips forward, slowly pushing myself through my hand.

Riley looked up at me, mouth open and eyes wide as he waited for me to...

"Fuck!" I growled as I fell back on my heels, my cock spurting in the air like a damn geyser.

The sounds of chimes and dings on the computer echoed, one after another.

I blinked through the heat, my muscles contracting as I continued to pump my shaft. My hand was covered in my release, as was my bed, my abs...

Good lord, I couldn't remember the last time I came this hard and this much.

I let go of my cock, my gaze falling on

the screen as I saw the comments.

All begging for my cum, my cock, and to be my good girl or good boy.

"Until next time, baby," I breathed, reaching forward to turn off the live recording manually like I always did.

When I was alone, I let out a deep breath, falling back onto my bed, my mind racing. I wiped my hand on the towel from my nightstand, trying to catch my breath.

I wasn't sure what happened. I hooked up with guys all the time, and I *never* once fantasized about them *during* a session. Or after we fucked in general. Most of them were mediocre at best.

Riley and I didn't even do anything!

My phone buzzed, and I moved to grab it, if only to put the ringer on silent, when I saw a notification that had nothing to do with my thirsty subs.

Would you like to have some fun tonight? Maybe grab some coffee?

The number was unknown, but I didn't have to be a private investigator to know who it was from.

Considering the emoji he'd sent was an eight ball.

Little shit.

I texted him back immediately with a pumpkin emoji.

You sure you won't turn into a pumpkin, Cinderella?

His response was instant.

Only if by pumpkin you mean pumpkin spice latte. Which in that case... yes.

A grin fell over my face.

What time? I asked.

Does 6 o'clock sound good? I work until 5.

I nodded, biting my bottom lip.

Sure. 6 sounds great.

When he texted mc back with a thumbs up, I couldn't help but panic.

While I was excited to see the object of my fantastical performance, I was also terrified. Like most people, it seemed Riley had a regular 9-5 gig, and me...

A date to a wedding didn't mean we were getting hitched.

I didn't *have* to tell him what I did for a living right?

I looked at my closet, acutely aware that this impression was everything. I wanted him to like me.

I wanted him to *want* to take me to the wedding of his own accord.

Ugh, he must have wacked me harder in the nuts than I thought. I can't remember ever mooning like this over... well, anyone.

Whatever, you're just having an off day, that's all.

At least, that was what I told myself as I shut down my bedroom studio, and headed to the bathroom for a shower.

CHAPTER SEVEN

Riley

I COULDN'T REMEMBER the last time I felt so nervous about just meeting someone for something as simple as coffee.

Though to be fair, Eric was right. If we were going to go to this wedding together, we should probably at least get to know one another a bit so it wouldn't be awkward. I'd given him the option to back out, but to my surprise he didn't.

Still, I felt like I was an awkward teenager all over again, waiting to meet my research partner at the library.

While secretly harboring a crush on

said partner.

Which was insane. I barely even *knew* Eric.

"Hey," his voice pulled me from my spiraling thoughts, and I turned to see him standing in front of me.

His dark hair fell in his sparkling blue eyes, perfectly pouty lips on display. He was just wearing a tight-fitting pair of jeans and a pumpkin-colored ringed baseball tee, but he looked like he'd literally stepped out of a magazine.

Yeah, I'm definitely out of my fucking league here.

"Hey," I said, rising from my chair, clearing my throat.

"Thanks for coming on such short notice." I moved toward the counter, Eric following me.

"Uh... yeah, of course," He said, his smooth voice like cinnamon butter on a fresh bagel.

"I'll have a large coffee. Black, please," I said to the cashier, nodding at Eric. "What do you want?" I asked.

Eric looked around as if I could be talking to anyone else. "I, uh..."

"It's the least I can do to make up for

yesterday," I said, my cheeks heating at the very memory of everything that went down yesterday.

The game, the audiobook... the fact I wanted to *kiss* him on his front porch.

I didn't go around kissing hot strangers. For God's sake, I didn't go around kissing anyone, if I was being honest.

So, the fact that Eric seemed to draw me in, the fact he made me want to do things I didn't usually do...

Yeah, I guess I had developed a crush.

Fuck me.

Eric smirked. "Well, if you insist, I'll have a large mocha latte with extra whip cream and sauce."

I watched as the cashier rang us up, handing the cups off to the barista as I paid.

By the time I was done, Eric had already grabbed our drinks and was waiting for me, looking just as hot as the damn beverages.

"I thought about what you said last night," I said as we took our seats.

Eric sat across from me, crossing his legs. The motion drew my attention to the definition of his form, the slender curve from thigh to knee, how his ankles tapered out into a larger foot.

I bet he would make a fantastic model to draw.

"You're going to have to be a little more specific, Cinderella. I said a lot of things," he teased, taking a sip of his drink. When he pulled back, I could see the faint hint of whip cream on his lip, and before I could say anything, his tongue darted out and swiped at it.

I wished I could say I wasn't so easy, but the truth of the matter was, I was as easy as pie.

The sight of him, licking any sort of frosted goodness off of those pouty lips was... sexy.

It made me think about him licking other... things...

I crossed my legs immediately as the image flitted through my mind, my cock twitching in agreement. I cleared my throat, burying myself in my own drink.

Pure, bitter, black coffee fixed everything. Especially unruly erections and existential crises.

"About having fun," I said, straightening my stature. I looked at him, his relaxed state, and I wished I could be like that.

Cool and sexy.

Instead, I was awkward at best where flirting was involved, and my life revolved around my job. Eric's suggestion that we actually hang out was intriguing to me not just because I wanted to get to know him, but also because I truly wanted to do something that was different. I didn't want to be a pumpkin anymore.

I wanted to be Cinderella at the ball, where she meets the prince of her dreams.

"Ah, I see. So, you thought you'd call me up and see what kind of trouble we could make together, is that it?" he said, flashing a grin, and I got the feeling trouble to him was much more than staying out late on a school night.

"I mean, unless you have other plans," I said, biting my bottom lip.

I watched as Eric drank from his cup again, spreading more of that delicious white cream all over his perfect lips.

Now is not the time, Riley!

Eric let out a laugh, the sound just as smooth as hot fudge on a sundae.

"Tell me, Riley, what do you *wish* you

could do? What do you like? And I swear to all that is holy, if you say *I don't know,* or *it's up to you,* you will eat those words." His tone was as aloof as it was dark, and I realized as his tongue darted out once more, sliding over his lips, that he was not just being cheeky. He was legit flirting with me.

Which made me even more self conscious.

"I, uh..." I cleared my throat again, trying to find the words. The truth was, I didn't know what I wanted to do.

Jasper Springs was a small town and there wasn't much to do there in general, and being as I didn't really spend my weekends traveling or visiting the city, I wasn't entirely sure what there was to do.

Or what normal folks did for fun.

My idea of fun involved getting messy with my canvas while I tuned out to my Spotify.

To just let go and... feel.

"Well, normally, I *like* to stay in and paint, but..."

"Painting, huh? Didn't peg you for an artist."

I knew I should have been offended

by his comment, after all, artists didn't have a *look*. Everyone was an artist, the mediums just differed. Some were more literal, like me and paint with traditional tools, while others painted digitally in Photoshop, or with words when they wrote. Some painted with flour and butter and sweet frosting, and others painted with cotton swabs and microscopes and proteins.

Everyone was an artist, because we all created something.

But something about his words felt less accusatory.

"I am. I teach art, actually."

I watched Eric's eyes widen, as if he was genuinely surprised, a flush of scarlet grazing his perfect complexion.

"I, uh... that's... wow. Can't say I was expecting that, although I guess that explains some things."

Before I could ask what the hell he meant, Eric shook his head, that same charming air returning once more.

"Okay, so I'm thinking maybe something a little less... introspective."

"Like what?" I asked, leaning my hand on my chin as I watched him intently.

"Well, seeing as you owe me a rematch, I was thinking maybe we could play some games..." He said the words smoothly, the corners of his lips turning up in a smirk.

"I would think you would be too wounded to be beaten again," I teased him, realizing the moment I'd said the words, I hadn't thought twice about them.

Being around Eric seemed to be bad for my control.

It was like I just couldn't help myself.

Eric's gaze darkened. "You got Lucky, Riley. That's it. Pure and simple. But I wasn't thinking pool..." he said, flipping his hair out of his eyes.

"Oh yeah, then what kind of game did you want to play with me, Eric?"

Eric grinned. "How about I pick you up tomorrow night at eight o'clock, and you can find out."

Tomorrow night. Eight o'clock. My insides tightened and I panicked, since eight pm was usually when I started winding down to get ready for bed, but I also knew that was what I wanted.

I wanted to change things, and change started with adding a little more... *fun* to my life.

But if I was being honest, I would have agreed to anything Eric proposed, even if it was a trip to Antarctica in the middle of January.

I bet he would look spectacular in a big puffy coat.

"Sounds good. I'll, uh, text you my address. Since I have your number and all," I said, blinking away the strange feeling that had settled over me, the nerves building in my stomach that screamed, "You're going to ruin this!"

I only hoped they weren't right.

CHAPTER EIGHT

Riley

BE THERE IN 5.

I stared at Eric's text, feeling the beginnings of sweat already to starting to form.

I'd gone through the entire day feeling nervous as all hell, and Chris's taunting didn't help. I knew he was just trying to ease my nerves, but I wasn't sure anything could take the edge off.

Nothing except probably a glass of wine, and I didn't think it was polite or good etiquette to drink *before* a date.

It's not a date.

It's just... hanging out.

With a really hot guy who you have a crush on and who's your plus one to a wedding.

As I delved further into a spiral of dread, my doorbell rang.

I took a deep breath, trying to calm my panic as I straightened my shoulders, heading toward the door. When I opened it, I had to focus on breathing.

For starters, Eric looked *divine*. Like sex on a freaking stick wearing a graphic tee that had some cartoon characters on it I had no idea who they were. But it was the ripped jeans, frayed at the knees, that *hugged* the man's thighs like a cradle and his shiny, perfectly spotless white tennis shoes that made him look like a polished magazine ad.

Mixed with his messy dark hair and bright blue eyes, and perfect jaw, I had to practically pick my mouth up off the floor.

It was a stark contrast to my dress pants and button down.

"Hi," he said, his voice like caramel, making my insides turn to molten lava again.

"Hey..." I said as I took in the sight of

him from head to toe.

"You ready for a night out on the town, Professor?" Eric said with a darkness that made my blood rush. Eric looked around me, at the inside of my house, and a part of me wanted to abandon this façade altogether, grab him by the collar and pull him in here and lock the door.

Mine, mine, mine.

The realization, the feeling, was overwhelming and foreign. I couldn't ever remember feeling this way about anyone, let alone this soon.

I nodded, shaking away the odd thoughts and feelings, instead focusing on the next right thing.

Just like Ana in Frozen, when I played it during class last winter.

"Yes," I said as I grabbed my keys, stepping outside. I locked the door quickly, following Eric down my steps toward his... BMW?

Shit, maybe he really is a kingpin.

That's okay, he can kidnap me any day.

Eric stepped up to the car, unlocking it with the remote, and I had to admit I was impressed. I didn't have keyless entry.

Eric casually strolled past me to open my door, and it was then I noticed the shiny watch on his wrist, glinting off the sheen of the car, which was also pristine.

"Age before beauty," he snickered, his lips turning up in the corner to reveal a perfect, white canine. I practically sunk into the seat because if I didn't, I'd have melted into a damn puddle on the ground.

"Thanks," I said as he rounded to the driver's side and climbed in.

When he'd started the car, I'd finally gotten my bearings and spoke up.

"So, uh, how old are you anyway?" I asked, trying not to sound like a complete perv, but also because I needed to know for my own sanity.

Plus Chris told me I needed to ask *real* questions because those led to conversations. He didn't understand my conversation skills were sorely lacking when it came to being in the same room with Mr. Perfect.

"Twenty-eight, why?"

"No shit," I said, realizing the moment I said it I sounded like a complete asshole.

Eric put the car in drive and pulled out of the driveway. "What?" he asked.

"You just... I would have thought you were a lot younger than that," I said, quickly recovering with, "Not that that's a bad thing. I mean, looking young is great, like really great, but, uh—"

Eric shook his head, a smile overtaking his lips. "Age isn't nothing but a number, Riley. Especially when it comes to... certain things." He cleared his throat. "Which you should know, being as you're..."

I could tell by the tone of his voice he wasn't offended. He was intrigued, and playing with me.

Which made me feel slightly more at ease, even if it was only a little.

"Thirty-eight," I squeaked.

Eric nodded in approval. "You look good for your age too, just so we're both on the same page," he said, letting out a dark chuckle. "But let's get something straight here, Riley Rabbit," he said, flashing me a smirk that made me warm all over. "Just because you're *older* doesn't make you wiser. And it certainly doesn't mean you're the one in charge," he said, taking his eyes off the road for a moment to cast a dirty look at me that brought my damn cock back to life.

No, no, no...

Not now!

"You understand?" he said, his voice dropping an octave, and I couldn't help the way I instantly responded, my voice full of desperation and need.

"Yes," I breathed.

Eric smirked, exposing that one perfect canine again, his shoulders squared, full of confidence.

"Yes, *Daddy*," he purred, and my entire being felt alive with electricity.

I don't know why I said the words.

It was like some spell, some invasion of the body snatchers bullshit.

My voice vomited the words of their own volition.

"Yes, Daddy," I said, with perfect dictation, my voice steady and strong.

"Good boy," Eric said as he turned back to the road, turning on the radio.

I internally chastised myself, my cock twitching at the thick tension in the BMW.

Fuck.

It's going to be a long night.

CHAPTER NINE

Eric

I DIDN'T KNOW what came over me, but the need to press Riley's buttons was driving me crazy.

That little *'yes, Daddy,'* was so easy to pull out of him, it was practically like taking candy from a baby.

Not to mention it had me harder than a slab of fucking marble.

The man was damn near *salivating* for some heavy praise, someone to take control and just...

Take it easy, Eric.

You just met the guy.

If you want things to be different, you

need to take it slow.

Otherwise, we might blow more than just Professor Good Boy's mind.

I pulled up to the parking lot of Wizard's Arcade & Grille, more than happy to have finally arrived. No sooner had I parked, was I out of the car.

I'd had every intention of opening Riley's door, like a fucking *gentlemen*, if only to show off that I too, could be prince charming.

I mean, my handle is Prince *Ayric.*

The slamming of the passenger door alerted me, and I nearly jumped, realizing he'd beaten me to it.

"An arcade?" he asked, almost as if he didn't believe it.

"Yeah... I mean, I did say we were going to be playing games," I said, noting the awe in his eyes.

I watched as Riley slid his hands into his pockets, turning toward me with a soft expression.

"I mean, I haven't been to an arcade since I was like, ten. I didn't even know these places still existed."

I nodded for him to follow me, feeling a bit pumped up at the moment that I'd chosen this place.

I had entertained the idea of taking him out to one of the many clubs in the city, but I wasn't sure how Mr. Perfect would react to shots and thumping bass for our first date, especially if he'd been on a strict curfew for awhile.

Not to mention, this isn't a date.

But even though I knew that, I couldn't help but let my fantasy build.

Maybe I wished it was.

God, I am so fucking off kilter today.

Well, technically ever since yesterday.

"Come on then, Cinderella. The ball awaits."

Inside Wizard's, the place was split into two sides. One side was lined with aqua leather booths and purple, mauve, and beige retro tables, white and mint green checkered floors giving the place a full on 50's meets 90's vibe. Combined with the sci-fi looking lamps and framed posters everywhere, it reminded me a lot of the mall I used to frequent as a kid.

On the other side of the grille was where all the fun happened. Rows and rows of arcade cabinets, pinball machines, and various dance machines brightly blinked and chirped, and there was even a console room with everything you could imagine if you wanted to have some more intimate one-on-one combat on the blow up neon furniture, or if you had a fantasy about getting caught with more than just your joystick in your hand.

I shook the dirty thoughts from my mind. I really was out of sorts.

I'd discovered this place when I did a photoshoot with Jordan and Sticky for the Jasper Springs Hotties calendar a few years back. Sticky ended up sick, and so, naturally, he called me in as his replacement, which was fine. It wasn't like I had anything going on anyway.

All that aside though, I'd come to be a bit of a fan of the place, and tried to come as often as I could, just to get away from the bullshit. All the marketing, the promotion, the planning of content on TikTok as well as my OF, the varied side gigs—like calendars and online boutiques among other things—sometimes, it was just nice to leave all of that shit at the door and just play some fucking games and overdose on sugar.

"Wow," Riley said, freezing in his spot, his gaze darting around the room taking it all in.

"You know if you actually want to have fun, you're going to have to move past the entryway," I taunted him, but I couldn't help but feel a warmth in my body at the way his lips curled in happiness, or the way his eyes sparkled like Willy Wonka had just given him the damn golden ticket.

"Right, I'm sorry—"

"Hey," I said, grabbing him by the arm, pulling him toward me. Riley followed my lead without question, and I couldn't deny how nice it was, his implicit trust.

But I stilled my own desires, instead choosing to focus on the task—and the man—at hand.

"Don't apologize," I said, dropping his arm.

Riley's dark eyes gazed down at me as he pursed his lips, nodding.

"I get that this is all a lot probably, but just know as long as you're with me, you don't need to explain shit. Just do what feels natural. Have fucking *fun*, and don't over think shit, okay?"

I wanted to touch him, to grab his hips and settle my hand at his back, dig my fingers into his skin.

But I knew *I* needed to take things slow and easy. I didn't want things to be awkward between us, not this fast.

Because honestly, I *liked* him. Something about his Sunday School-Sweet-As-Pie Professor vibe was really fucking doing it for me, and I didn't just want to play with him like a pristine GI Joe.

I wanted him to like *me.* I wanted him to *want* to take me to the wedding, and maybe I wanted him to think I was more than just some guy he met in a bar who lost a bet. Maybe I wanted to be Cinderella, for once.

I couldn't explain where these strange ideas or feelings were coming from, so instead of delving into a spiral, I gently pressed my hand to his back, urging him on.

"Well, big boy, it's your party, so pick the first game," I said as I queued up the QR code on my phone.

I'd been a VIP at Wizards for a little over two years and had accumulated way more credits than I'd ever use.

Guess I finally found a good use for them.

Riley walked through the aisles, and I

followed, watching as the neon glow lit him up like some lost character from Tron.

Finally, after walking around for what felt like ten minutes, he stopped, pointing toward the center of the arcade room in the round robin.

"That one," he said nodding to the large, three paneled screen of Pac Man.

"Pac Man, really? That's what you're going with?" I asked, surprised he would have gone for the digital version and not the vintage cabinet a few rows over.

"What's—"

I shot him a glance, reminding him there was no apologies here.

"Yes, that *is* my choice," he said, like a petulant teenager.

His tone was so perfectly *bratty*, I had to put my fist in my damn mouth just to still the twitch in my palm, the overwhelming desire to bend him over the player console and smack the attitude right out of him.

I bet he'd like it too.

"All right then," I said as I scanned my QR code for credit, and he took his stance.

"I'm going to get us some drinks," I

said as he used the touch pad to make the little yellow guy chomp his way through the little blinking circles.

I watched the faint muscles in his forearm tighten as he tapped the buttons with precision and quickness.

"Sounds good," he said, flashing a smile as he focused on the screen.

CHAPTER TEN

Eric

THIS SEEMS TO be a pattern with us.

Riley fist bumped the air as he grinned widely. After two rounds of drinks, and more than enough games of Pac Man, I'd finally settled on my choice of challenge for the night.

Air Hockey.

"I'm starting to think you are just a sore loser," Riley chuckled.

I shot him a glare as I queued up my code for the scan credit.

"I've never been a fan of Pac Man, to tell you the truth. I'm much more of a Galaga guy."

Riley smirked as he took his stance on the end of the table, the whizzing of the air from the puck spout pulling my attention.

"Are you even old enough to know Galaga?" he taunted, but the words carried a hint of insecurity.

"I'm old enough to kick your ass and make you beg for mercy," I said, slamming the puck down on the plastic field. I took my spot.

"I'd like to see you try," Riley said with a grin.

It was a blur of neon, a symphony of air and crashing goals as we both steadily kept up our defense.

Slam!

The sound of the puck and the loud buzzer sounded as my goal was scored.

"Yes!" I bit out. "I'm coming for you, baby," I said, a grin spreading on my face.

Riley only hunkered down more, his frame like a monster, his gaze hungry to *win.*

"Beginner's luck" he said, licking his lips.

The sight caused my cock to twitch as he slammed the puck down once more, whipping it toward me, directly into my goal.

"Fuck!" I growled, grabbing the puck as Riley *brattily* squared his shoulders, nodding to me cockily.

"You were saying?" he taunted.

I slid the puck back with force as he tried to block me. But it was no use. This was my favorite game at Wizards, and I'd grown up playing it in my parent's basement.

There was no way I was going to let him beat me at my own game. My goal rang, and I smiled wickedly.

"I said, I am *coming for you*, Riley. Tonight, I will own you."

Riley aimed another shot, and I managed to block him. We were officially tied.

He grunted in annoyance, and I had to admit the change of tone, the undercurrent of *brat* on him was making me damn near salivate.

I whipped the puck back, angling from the side, and it slid in with ease.

Riley cursed, throwing his arms in the air. But we still had two points left until the game would be over.

The next shot from Riley was so

fierce, the damn puck flew off the table. I caught it before it hit the ground.

"Nice try," I said, slamming it back down, hitting it with precision as it struck its goal, seamlessly.

"Fucking hell," he breathed, now visibly shaken. One point left, and he was mine.

"Should we sweeten the stakes?" I asked, licking my lips, knowing full well I had this in the bag.

"Really, Eric? *Now* you want to be all cute and cocky?" he said, slamming the puck down, setting his shuttle on top of it. His gaze bore into mine like a fire, imploring me to flinch. But flinch I would not.

"Winner chooses the next date," I said with a smile. A part of me wanted to immediately erase the word, which I hadn't meant to say, but before I could, Riley shot his puck directly into my goal.

Fuck!

I breathed in deep. This was it, the tie breaker. The moment of truth.

His steady gaze held mine, unwavering.

I let out a deep breath as I held his gaze, and took my shot.

Riley stopped it, slamming his shuttle on top of the puck and shucking it back at me from an angle. The puck bounced like a pinball off the sides, and I tried to stop it, its momentum building with each ricochet.

And just as I went to block, the contact and the air pushed it right into my goal.

Fuck!

Fury ignited me, heating my insides once more. I flashed my gaze up at him, to see the shock and awe on his face, watched as it spread into a grin that was somehow childish but also sexy as fuck.

I tossed the shuttle down as I stalked over to him, standing tall against his frame.

Riley smiled down at me smugly, touting the brattiest, "I win," I'd ever heard. He settled his hand on my hip, his lips turning up into a warm, victorious grin.

The feel of his palm against my hip, burning through the fabric of my shirt was damn near electric.

"Fuck you," I breathed, feeling overwhelmed by the sight of this man. Of his warm eyes, of his heated touch, of the way I wanted nothing more than to fall into him like a damn meteorite.

Riley leaned in a fraction, his lips inches away from mine.

"Eric…"

I didn't miss the way his Adam's apple bobbed, or the maddening hardness pressed against me. Instinctively, I slid my hand up his trim, solid chest, over his back. His pulse thrummed beneath my fingertips, and I found it hard to focus on anything except the one thought in my brain.

Kiss him.

CHAPTER ELEVEN

Riley

I COULDN'T REMEMBER the last time I had so much *fun*. Not only that, but I couldn't remember the last time I won anything on my own. I'd won several games of Pac Man, and defeated Eric at air hockey, which I had to admit was one hell of a game, but as I looked down at Eric, his hand settled on my hip, eyes ablaze, I felt like I was winning at far more than games.

And thanks to the drinks, I felt like for the first time, maybe I had something *fun* of my own to offer.

Eric seemed to bring out a part of me

I didn't know existed, and I wanted more of that.

I wanted more of *him*.

Overwhelmed by his sparkling gaze, I knew all it would take, was one swift move and I could have him. He was so close.

My gaze dipped to his perfect mouth, the one that sounded so good talking shit, that was parted just the slightest.

Maybe it was the alcohol. Maybe it was the fact Eric looked hot as hell amid the neon glow of Wizard's.

Or maybe it was that I had lost my marbles completely.

I leaned in just a fraction, but our lips would never touch.

Because mere seconds later, someone was calling my name.

"Mr. Evans?"

Instantly, the spell was broken, and I dropped my hand, moving away from Eric, scanning the room to see who was calling my name, and where they were.

When my gaze finally settled on the culprit, my eyes widened.

Trent Klaypas, one of my students from Senior Painting, waved at me.

A quick glance at my watch told me it

was only ten-thirty, which immediately set off my teacher brain.

What was he doing out so late on a school night?

Come to think of it, maybe we should get going.

"Hey..." I said nervously, feeling myself start to sweat.

"What are you doing all the way out here?" he asked, tugging on his backpack.

"I could ask you the same question, young man," I said, with a forced grin.

Trent laughed as he nodded to the bar. "I work in the kitchen. Dishwasher. Just on my way home," he said, looking back and forth between Eric and I.

"Oh, where are my manners?" I said, running a hand through my hair.

"Eric, this is Trent, one of my students. Senior Painting."

I watched as Eric's jaw tensed, his entire body stiffening. He held his hand out, and Trent took it. He appraised Eric like a specimen.

Did they know one another?

"Nice to meet you," Eric said politely, flashing a grin that was rather fake, but charming nonetheless.

"Yeah, *pleasure's* all mine," Trent said with a wink, and I watched as they dropped hands, and Eric shoved his in his pockets.

"Well, anyway, I'm heading out, I just wanted to say *hey*. See you in class tomorrow," he said, flashing a grin, and I waved.

When he was gone, I let out a sigh. "I know it's probably early for you, but—"

"Turning into a pumpkin already?" Eric said, his voice the same, smooth sound that made my insides melt, but something was off. He sounded... sad, almost.

Guilty.

But that was probably my imagination.

What would Eric have to feel guilty about?

"Yeah," I said, running a hand through my hair.

"I mean, it *is* a school night," I said sheepishly.

Eric nodded as he took the lead, and I followed.

The entire way home, he was quiet. The tension in the air was thick, and I was out of my mind wondering if I'd done something, said something.

If it was because we'd almost kissed.

If it was because we *hadn't* kissed.

For a moment, I thought I'd overreacted. Read too much into his attitude. His perfect lips...

"Well, Cinderella, better get you inside before the clock strikes twelve," he said finally as we pulled up to my house.

I nodded, letting out a sigh, the both of us quiet and still for a moment. Eric opened his door. I did the same.

"What are you doing?" I asked as I walked around in front of the BMW.

"Being a gentleman," Eric snapped, his tone slightly annoyed.

"You don't have to—"

"Yeah, well, maybe I want to," he said, his shoulders stiffening. "Maybe I want to be prince charming for once," he muttered.

Something about his words stirred something deep within me. Both a desire to placate and soothe as well as submit.

"Okay..." I said, much more breathlessly than I cared to admit.

Eric walked me to my door, and I fumbled with my keys. I didn't want him to leave, but...

The moment he turned away, to head back to his car, I couldn't help myself. I grabbed him by the arm, stopping him in his tracks. I decided at that moment, that I didn't want him to leave without knowing how I felt.

How he made me feel.

I'd been on a lot of dates in my life, but none had ever felt so... right.

"Eric," I started.

He turned, looking at me with bright blue eyes, full of wonder and dare I say hope?

"Yeah?" he breathed, his voice only shaking the slightest.

"I... I had a really great time tonight," I said, licking my lips. Sweat broke out on my forehead, and I could feel my insides swirling like a hurricane.

Eric swallowed, flashing me a genuine smile that was both endearing and wistful. And I was powerless to fight the feeling. I was powerless to fight the connection between us.

Eric fell into my space, and I fell into him with ease, pulling him close.

I slid my hand in his hair, tilting his face up to mine as I crushed my lips against his.

A part of me half expected him to pull away, but he didn't. Instead, he melted against me like warm butter on toast, groaning with a deep satisfaction that echoed in my mouth, bringing my cock back to life once more.

I gripped the edge of his hair with my fingers as I relaxed, relishing in the warmth of his skin against my palm, of his tongue in my mouth, caressing mine.

Eric kissed me like he was starving. Like he *needed* me as much as I needed him.

When he pulled away, I spoke. "I'd likc to see you again. If... if that's okay, and you're free, I mean," I hurried, feeling a monumental weight as I said the words.

"I'd like that," Eric said, licking his pouty lips, which were beautifully swollen still from kissing me. His voice was like fudge, thick and rich. He walked away slowly.

"I mean, I did win the game," I said, smiling wide.

Eric appraised me with his gaze as he stopped halfway to the car.

"Right. Of course," he said, waving at me as he turned around.

I watched from my porch as he got in his sleek car, pulled out, and drove away.

Only once the door was locked, did I let out a breath of relief, a smile curling at the edges of my lips. I fist bumped the air like a total dork, like I too, was a teenager.

A teenager who'd gotten lucky with the hottest guy in school.

My mind was spinning, reeling from our night, our kiss.

One look at the clock on the stove told me it was nearing eleven thirty, and I knew I needed to get to bed soon.

Normally, I'd shower in the morning, but I was also usually in bed by now, so I knew it would be best to shower before bed so I could grab a few extra snoozes in the morning.

I undressed on my way to the bathroom, tossing my clothes in the hamper. Turning on the shower, I let the water run for a moment, waiting for it to warm. My cock throbbed, stiff as a board, and instinctively, I ran my hand along the length. Warm, sticky bits of precum lined my slit, and I let out a frustrated groan, remembering Eric's contented sound, his tongue in my mouth.

I let go of myself as I entered the warm spray, trying to push the images in my mind away. I needed to get cleaned up, needed to get to bed, so I could get up on time.

But the ache in my balls, and the solidness of my throbbing erection were too much, and I knew there was only one way to truly quiet my need.

I slid my wet hand over my shaft slowly, my hips thrusting of their own accord. Bracing myself against the wall with my free hand, I closed my eyes, focusing only on the feel of my hand, the motion. It'd been a long time since I felt *anyone* else's touch, and I'd grown content with that. At least, I thought I had.

But soon my mind filled with the memory of Eric once more, of my fingers in his hair, of his deep, throaty groans, of his warm tongue caressing mine.

Of his hardness pressed against me.

Slowly, I dragged myself out of my warm, wet palm, a deep groan escaping my throat.

I imagined we didn't stop there, on

my porch.

I imagined my lips caressed that sweet corner of his mouth, the spot where his smirk sat as he gazed up at me. I imagined sliding my hands over his hips, along the curve of his ass in his sexy jeans, over his hardness.

I thrust myself through my fist once more, this time picking up the pace as I imagined the sounds he'd make beneath me, the way his hands would feel touching me the way I wanted to touch him.

I imagined the warmth of his needy mouth wrapped around my swollen cock, and letting out a frustrated groan.

My hips thrust harder, faster as the image of Eric before me—no, *beneath* me—perfect, pouty lips wrapped around me, sucking, licking...

"Fuck!" I growled as I came, hard.

My stomach muscles tightened as I hazily opened my eyes, watching my cock spray the wall with my release, with an intensity I'd never felt before.

I stroked myself slowly, trying to catch my breath as my release continued to spurt and I emptied myself. The water had gone cold when I'd finally gone soft, and I couldn't deny I felt different.

But it was a good sort of different.

Like everything was changing, and for once, I was looking forward to tomorrow.

CHAPTER TWELVE

Eric

WHAT THE HELL am I doing?

I tossed my keys on the counter.

Why do I always want things I can't fucking have?

Granted, I knew more than anyone that someone's job didn't define them, but I couldn't deny the panic that laced through me the moment Riley told me he was a fucking *high school* teacher.

No wonder he was the star of my professor fantasy.

College teacher?

Sure, I could handle that. College was a lot more lenient with shit than fucking high school, I knew that first hand.

I hadn't disclosed my occupation, and now I was more worried than ever that discussing such a topic would more than likely torpedo everything. Cue *Bye Bye Bye* playing in the background and I'd never see Riley again.

I thought for sure I was going to lose my shit when his fucking *student* recognized me.

Which also made me feel guilty as hell.

Was he one of my regular subs or a casual lookie loo?

Was he even legal?

Christ, the night had gone from zero to sixty way too fucking fast.

There were a million questions floundering through my brain, and I needed to not think.

I needed to shower, and get the fuck to sleep and maybe then, in the morning when I was more clear, I'd be able to process how I was going to handle the situation. In the morning I could be the smart, better man.

But right now, all I could do was lick my lips, savoring the taste of Riley for just a moment longer.

Fuck me.

I removed my clothes, feeling all too constrained. My cock throbbed from the memory of his kiss, the taboo-ness of our situation.

I turned the shower on, making it as cold as I could, if only to stifle the maddening erection I'd sprung.

The thought of *being caught* spiraled into being caught by my *hot professor date*, and cold water wasn't doing anything.

"Fuck!" I barked as I slammed my fist against the tile. I knew I needed to put Riley, and everything around him out of my mind, but the truth was I couldn't stop thinking about him. How much fun we'd had together, how sweet and... hot... it was when he grabbed me and kissed me like some Princess in a fairytale. Telling me he wanted to see me again.

My fleshlight mount rattled from my slamming the tile, and my gaze diverted to the answer.

Typically, I liked to edge myself a bit prior to my daily posts, if only because it made the experience and the filming more accurate, but that didn't mean I didn't pleasure myself off screen from time to time. Though my own self-love sessions had taken a stark backseat to my filmed ones, because it was easier to feel less alone with a thousand people watching me come. When it was just me, my hand, and a sea of subscribers, I could pretend better.

But alone, in my shower, with a cock harder than Thor's hammer, the overwhelming desire to *pretend* was irrefutable.

I slid my hand over my cock, spreading the water along the sensitive thickness of my shaft. The touch alone made my cock twitch, and I squeezed my head, running my thumb through my wet slit. My gaze focused on the mount in front of me, and I supposed I garnered it was a means to an end. It didn't *mean* anything.

Tomorrow, I'd deal with the truth, with destroying everything.

But now??

What would a little fantasy hurt, right?

I let go of my cock, smacking it just a bit to watch it bob back and forth. The need to *fuck* something was intense, especially with my favorite toy only inches away.

But it wasn't the warm, plush walls of my Fleshlight I really wanted. It was Professor Hot Stuff, on his fucking knees before me.

I closed my eyes as I let the image fill my brain, of him and his long legs tucked underneath him, hands flat on his thighs as he gazed up at *me*, begging *me*. Mouth open, waiting for my cock.

For me to fill his fucking mouth with my cum until it dripped out of the corners of his precious, fuckable mouth.

"That's it," I purred in the sanctity of my bathroom as I lined myself up, brushing my leaking head against the entrance of my toy.

I smacked it with my head, the wobbly texture of the Fleshlight jiggling as I did so, and I imagined it was his mouth, fighting for a taste.

"Open wide for Daddy," I murmured as I shoved myself in, letting the plush silicone walls encompass my aching cock. It didn't take long for me to build a rhythm. I braced both hands against the tile wall, picturing the way his lips wrapped around my thickness, letting my mind wander. The memory of feeling of his tongue against mine spurred thoughts of his tongue rolling around my head. I thrust harder, faster, needing to feel the warmth, his mouth sucking me, licking me.

God, it felt so fucking good.

Harder.

Faster.

I imagined him draining me of every last drop of cum I had, then teaching me a fucking lesson.

You're going to pay for that, he purred in my fantasy.

Another hard thrust, and my fucking mount slipped off as I pulled out, falling to the ground.

"Fuck!" I roared, my release so close I could taste it.

I knew it would take a minute to reposition everything, and I wasn't sure I had the focus or capacity to do so.

I needed to fucking come. I needed to put Professor Hot stuff out of my mind. I needed to fuck this out of my system.

I grabbed my Fleshlight from the ground, taking matters into my own hands once more.

Make me, I touted in my cerebral

fantasy, the scent of my release prevalent in the air as he breathed his words into my ears. I turned over as I imagined him touching me, forcing me to give him my ass.

And then I came, hard and fast, my entire body spasming with release at the very *thought* of him punishing me.

Like the dirty little whore I was.

Daddy is a dirty little whore.

As soon as the relief came, so did the shame.

The guilt.

Because I knew it would only be a fantasy.

That's all it could ever be.

CHAPTER THIRTEEN

Riley

MY PHONE BUZZED incessantly as I stuffed down my first bite of my chicken salad. One glance at the screen showed it was my brother, Aaron.

Heads up we're heading out this weekend to check out a couple clubs for the bach party.

Shit!

I'd almost completely forgotten!

Technically, I was the best man and the bachelor party was my wheelhouse, but my brother and his friends all knew I was not the best choice when it came to partying, and I wanted my brother to have the best night, so we'd all agreed to choose a place after scouting out locations *together*. That way, I could oversee the finer details while also being sure that the place we picked was something up to Aaron's caliber.

Before I could answer, Chris came waltzing through the door, lifting himself to sit on my demo counter, swinging his legs back and forth as he giddily pressed me to tell him how my *date* went, so getting back to my brother would have to wait.

"It wasn't a date," I reminded him as I took another stab at my salad.

"Were you in bed before nine o clock?" he teased.

"No, of course not. I—"

"Did you have drinks? Flirt a little? Maybe even get a little first base action?" Chris challenged, using his hands to mold and grope the air like a seventh grader.

I couldn't help the heat that formed in my cheeks at his insinuation, and that was telling enough.

"Oh my God, you did!" he teased, and I threw down my fork in defense.

"It wasn't like that, it was... it was..."

"Riley and Mafia Man sitting in a tree—"

"Stop!" I said, unable to control my laughter.

Chris only wriggled his eyebrows at me with a smile. "Hey, all I'm saying is you deserve to have a little fun you know," Chris said through his own laugh. "So where'd he take you?"

I smiled as I recalled the previous night. "Some arcade in the city, called Wizards."

Chris raised an eyebrow. "I know that place. They're like Dave and Busters on Pop Rocks."

It was my turn to raise an eyebrow. "Pop Rocks?"

Chris rolled his eyes, his tone mimicking the valley girl accent that perpetuated the films of our youth.

"Well, we *are* an anti-drug district, Mr. Evans, crack is wack. And so nineteen eighty."

I scoffed in return as I stabbed my salad.

"I, uh, actually ran into a student there," I admitted. "Wasn't sure what to say, you know, like how to introduce him or anything, so I just said like, hey this is my friend and this is one of my students... like a lame teacher."

Chris let out a laugh. "Hope you weren't in a compromising position," he teased.

Heat rushed my face again as I remembered being so close to Eric, wanting to kiss him right then and there.

I let my head fall onto my desk, hiding the flush I knew was covering my cheeks.

"I am so screwed," I murmured. I'd only had a couple drinks, but the lord knew how teenagers talked.

It wasn't like I was completely in the closet, but I didn't really share my personal life with my students. Not that I had much of a social life to share to begin with, but still...

Most of the staff knew I was gay, but it wasn't like there was a neon sign outside my door.

"Looks like you won't be dancing on your own at the wedding after all," Chris said as my phone chimed again because I hadn't closed out the notification.

I lifted my head, if only to grab my phone and silence the notification.

"Lover boy texting you already? Wanting some of that grade A Evans di—"

"Oh my God, Chris, stop! No, it's my brother. We're doing the club scout this weekend. You know, where we're supposed to go into the city and find the perfect pen of debauchery or whatever..."

"You should invite Lover Boy. I bet he'd be down to get low or whatever it is the kids are calling it these days," Chris said, sticking his tongue out and making metal head signs with his fingers.

"I..."

I hadn't really thought about *inviting* anyone because, truth be told, I hadn't *had* anyone to invite, until now.

Come to think of it, I *did* win the last game, and the winner got to pick the next date.

Certainly, my brother wouldn't object.

Just as I contemplated Chris's words, the lunch bell rang, and I realized I hadn't even finished my salad.

Damn it!

"Ah, well, that's my cue, Romeo. Catch up with you and that Grade A later," Chris called over his shoulder, his hand hitting the top of the door pane on his way out.

I sighed as the students filed into the room, vowing that during class time today I'd finish my lunch the way it was intended, and perhaps, I would take the initiative to invite Eric out this weekend.

CHAPTER FOURTEEN

Riley

I CASUALLY SKETCHED out a bust on my paper, if only because I needed to keep my hands busy while the rest of my students worked on their still-lifes.

I'd stared at the current set up of flowers and vases and reflective objects long enough, not to mention my brain kept replaying last night over and over. That moment on my porch, where Eric looked up at me with hope and wonder.

Like he could see *me.* And not just the me that towered over him, but the me I hadn't realized I'd lost.

Slowly, I shaded in the clavicle,

adding shadows to the neck and side of the head, cross-hatching the bust into more of a silhouette.

By the time the bell rang, I had Eric's facial features sketched in, albeit they were mostly visible via the shadows.

"Remember, your projects are due Friday!" I said, assuming my authority again as everyone started packing up.

"So, those of you who need art passes, make sure you see me no later than tomorrow morning!" I announced, though as usual, no one took me up on the offer.

I turned around to clean up the remains of my lunch, when a voice pulled me from my thoughts.

"Did you... uh... have a good time last night?" I turned around to see Trevor, tugging on his bookbag.

"Trevor, hey... I, uh... yeah, I had a great time. With... my... friend. My friend, Eric," I said awkwardly, almost word vomiting.

Trevor shook his head with a grin. "I know it's none of my business but, uh, it's just... I didn't think you were into guys..." he said hurriedly, recovering with, "Like Eric. I mean, it's cool if you are but, like, I just..."

"Trevor, I—"

"I mean, you seem like a really nice guy—for like, an old guy—"

Old guy?

I'm only thirty-eight for fucks sake!

I'm not dead!

"I'm thirty-eight!" I said in alarm. "I'm not—"

"I know. I mean, I don't know, but I know, I mean... ugh, why is this so hard?" Trevor said, his cheeks turning red.

I wasn't sure what Trevor was getting at it by his comment, and a part of me was surprised he'd confronted me in general. Though he was a great student with a lot of artistic potential, we didn't *talk* about his social interactions or things outside of school during his study hall sessions when he'd come in to work on his projects.

The flush on his cheeks, the chewing of the lip... the way he was dancing around the topic... Suddenly, I realized the subtext of what he was saying.

Trevor himself was gay. And likely hadn't told anyone.

"Trevor, if this is about what you

think you saw... If you are feeling... some sort of way—"

"Oh God, no!" Trevor said shaking his head. "I mean, I like you, but not like that, obviously. Not that you're not attractive, or... Oh my God, what I mean is just..."

I swallowed harshly at his trail of compliments, because even as nice as they were, they were certainly misplaced.

"I just wanted to tell you to be careful, that's all. You seem like a good guy... I think, and I just don't want to see some asshole hurt you."

My heart sank at his words.

For starters, Eric was the furthest thing from an asshole, and why on earth would he hurt me?

"I appreciate your concern, Mr. Klaypas, but my personal life is just that. My *personal* life. There is a reason I don't share it. Because I value my privacy," I said as politely as I could.

"But if you need someone to talk to about anything, you know you can talk to me," I said as nicely as I could. I knew how hard it was growing up in this town; after all, I'd been a lot like Trevor once myself.

Trevor sighed, nodding. "Yeah, right of course, my bad. I just... I'm sorry, can... can we pretend this never happened?" he asked, his flush returning to normal. A part of me understood his desire to forgo the awkwardness, and clam up. Perhaps whatever was truly bothering him, he wasn't ready to divulge to himself.

"Of course," I said, for I too, wanted nothing more than to forget this equally embarrassing moment.

"Okay, well... um, in that case, I'm gonna go..."

I wrote him his art pass, sent him on his way, and tried to shake off the odd encounter.

Glancing at the clock, I knew I only had ten minutes left until the buses would clear out, which meant if I *wanted*, I could leave early.

I usually stayed around till at least six, working on curriculum and getting everything organized for my professional development and the upcoming field trip as well as organizing my things for next week's project. But as I looked out the window at the sun shining down on the pavement, as I watched the kids walking outside, goofing off, I felt a need to shirk my adult responsibilities and just do something fun.

Maybe I'd catch a movie—something I hadn't done in awhile—or swing by the cafe for a coffee, or even just go for a walk.

The world was full of endless possibilities, and so I didn't waste a moment as I grabbed my phone, my jacket, and headed out into the world anew.

CHAPTER FIFTEEN

Eric

I STARED AT the text that read *Brunch?*

I hadn't seen Julie since the other night, when the guys and I met up at M's Place. The night I first met Riley.

Even though it was almost a week ago now, it felt like ages.

To be honest, I hadn't thought about much else except Riley, and the fact that I could feel myself falling into his quicksand.

It was hard not to like him, once you got past his Sunday School attire and his blushing cheeks.

And he does play a good game of air

hockey.

I decided that maybe a good brunch was what I needed to get my head right, to get myself back on track.

I needed to come clean to Riley about my job, about who I really was, if only because I knew it would come back to bite me in the ass if I didn't. I hated lying, and I wasn't ashamed of what I did.

But I worried that coming clean would be a deal breaker for Sunday's Best Professor, and I didn't want to think about the reality that my truth might push him away. Like it pushed others away.

So, instead of thinking about derailed fairytales, I answered Julie with a *sure.*

When I arrived at *Rose & Evelyn's,* Jasper Springs's "upscale" spot—which was about as upscale as a *Red Lobster,* Julie was already waiting, mimosa in hand.

"Good morning," she said with a grin, twirling her flute.

"Afternoon," I said, flashing her with a grin of my own. "It is eleven am, you're already drinking, and this is brunch, so I think we're well past morning."

Julie smiled as the waitress came by, and I put my coffee order in.

I barely had a look at the menu before Julie was off.

"It's five o'clock somewhere, darling," she said with a kissy face that made me roll my eyes.

"So, how did it go the other night?" she asked sweetly.

I peered up at her from my menu. "What?" I asked, feeling self-conscious all of a sudden. I hadn't mentioned to anyone about my date-not-date with Riley, but that didn't mean Julie couldn't have known. The woman had an uncanny knack for gossip and was often in the places you least expected her. It would be just like her to spot me in a compromising position, only to bring it up later.

"I mean, it's not every day someone beats you at a game of pool," she said, sipping her drink again.

Oh, of course... M's Place... the other night.

"Uh, yeah, I know. It's crazy, right?" I asked, breathing a sigh of relief. "It was fine. I guess. Riley gave me a ride home. Got all embarrassed when his smutty audiobook came on over the speakers. Was kind of funny actually." I chuckled at the memory.

"Shut up! He did not!" Julie exclaimed, her eyes wide, faced filled with excitement.

I shook my head, my own grin spreading across my face. It felt good to laugh, to just let out the things that had been rolling around in my head.

"We, uh, actually hung out the other night too. Had a good time."

Julie's face was practically glowing. "I knew it," she said, beaming with pride.

"What are you talking about?" I asked, and took a sip of my coffee.

"I knew you two would hit it off," she said as the waitress came by to take our orders.

After putting in for a tower of cinnamon spice pancakes, I did not relent.

"What the fuck are you talking about, Jules?"

Julie shrugged, smirking at me over her mimosa. "Oh nothing, just saying that's why I arranged the blind date in the first place. I had a feeling you two would get along," she shrugged.

What?
Is she saying...

"Riley... he was the guy you tried to set me up with? The one who blew me—"

"Well, not even fate could keep you two apart, it seemed. I mean, you did still both show up at M's Place—completely of your own accord, might I add—"

"I don't fucking believe this," I said, feeling a fresh wave of panic.

He was the guy who stood me up!

Julie dismissed my shock with a wave.

"Why didn't you say somcthing the other night—"

Julie shrugged. "Maybe I just wanted to see how you two played out on your own."

"Un fucking believable," I said, downing my coffee.

"What?"

"You didn't think..." I said as I looked around, keeping my voice low. "You didn't think my job would be an issue?" I asked, raising my eyebrow at her.

"Why would it be?" she asked, cocking her head to the side. "I told him you worked in social media, that's not a lie."

"Oh, I don't know, Jules, maybe because I fucking get naked for a living and he melds the minds of today's youth," I growled.

Julie's eyebrows furrowed. "Since when has taking off your pants for a living bothered you? You're the one who's always saying—"

"It doesn't, but—"

"But what? Clearly something has your briefs all in a twist."

I sighed, just as the waitress dropped our food off. I stabbed my pancake much harder than I'd intended, the metal of the silverware chiming loudly off the plate.

"You of all people know how many people have had an *issue* with what I do. And none of them were *teachers*."

"So, no nude modeling then for the art class, got it," she teased.

I grunted in response as I stuffed some pancake in my mouth, the sickeningly sweet syrup thick on my tongue.

Julie's gaze softened. "I do know what you mean, you know. But I also know that Riley is one of the most accepting people on the planet. He's a good guy, Eric. I promise."

"Yeah, that's the fucking problem, Julie. He's *good*. And I'm..."

I couldn't finish my sentence, because I knew the truth that awaited. Riley was good, and I was a sin that would forever stain him, and the last thing I wanted was to ruin someone as perfect as him.

So I buried my heartache in my syrup and butter, because it was turning out to be quite a shitty morning.

CHAPTER SIXTEEN

Eric

AFTER THE BOMBSHELL Julie had dropped on me at brunch, I'd wanted nothing more than to put Riley out of my mind once and for all, but I couldn't stop thinking about the fact that he'd stood me up.

Not intentionally, I'm sure. Riley didn't seem the type to have a menacing bone in his body, but it still felt like a punch to the gut.

Another punch I wasn't prepared for.

It was like the universe was trying to push me toward the man when I was more than certain the truth would tear us apart.

Fuck, why is shit so damn complicated?

I decided instead to focus on my upcoming daily post. For years, my job had been more of a comfort than a burden. In the beginning, it was just something I did for fun, for attention, and in some ways it still was, but somewhere along the line it became more than just fun, it became a habit, a job.

One that paid pretty well, and didn't require a lot.

And now, it was the only constant in my life. Every day, on the dot, I got to tap out of life, I got to forget.

Forget about my loneliness, about my non-existent relationships.

I adjusted my lights once more, making sure my bed was set up and I had everything I needed.

Lube.

Toys.

A well positioned camera.

It was the same every time, and I liked to be prepared, in case I wanted to switch things up. I lay back on my soft sheets, my head against the pile of pillows as I got comfortable. Palming my cock through my briefs, I tried my best to clear my mind.

I focused on the feel of my cock, solid beneath my briefs, the sensation of all the blood in my body finding its way to the center of me. I lazily rubbed my stiffness, biting my lip as I contemplated where I wanted this session to go. Where I needed it to go so I could forget.

The familiar sound alerted me that I'd started recording, but I didn't open my eyes yet. I formed a picture in my brain as I rubbed myself, thrusting my brief covered cock against my hand, and immediately pulled away.

Not yet.

I opened my eyes, making eye contact with the camera. I'd done this "oops you caught me" scenario more than once, and every time I did, the subs loved it. In the past, I'd gotten off on being watched, but now, getting off was just...

It didn't feel the same anymore. It felt empty, despite the fact thousands were watching me, waiting for me to come for them.

A quick glance at the comments coming in live only cemented the truth.

And for a moment, I wished he was watching.

Professor Hot Stuff.

What a show I could give him...

I knelt up on my knees, palming my briefs once more, making eye contact and asking them how bad they wanted to see my cock. How bad they wanted me to fuck their mouths, or their asses.

The resounding sound of tips and comments flooded along with my fantasy as I stared at the screen, pretending it wasn't me and a thousand people.

I looked into that camera, and despite my best efforts to do otherwise, I could only envision it was *him* watching me.

I slid my briefs down, letting my cock spring free. Arching my back for more thrusting, I let my hand trace over my thickness, feeling the sticky precum already coating my head.

I peered down at the screen, reading the comments. People said the most depraved, dirty things when they thought no one was watching.

One request caught my eye, and I garnered perhaps it would be better to let them lead me, so my fantasy didn't stray. If I was giving the viewers what they wanted, I could chalk it up to business.

What I wanted didn't factor in the equation, because what I wanted...

I pushed the thought out of my mind as I smirked for the camera, removing the rest of my underwear as I got off the bed, walking over to my nightstand with the toys.

I wasted no time picking out the thickest cock in my collection, along with some warming lube.

The request to watch me come while I got fucked wasn't an abnormal one, but it wasn't something I preferred to do for the cameras often.

Mostly because in love and in life, I was the one who preferred to do the fucking.

But I'd realized then that maybe it was what I needed to forget about Riley, forget about the things that would undoubtedly disappear the moment reality was back at hand.

I made a show of slathering the twelve inch *Big Daddy* cock in copious amounts of lube, slowly rubbing and squeezing my hands along the veiny silicone shaft I held beneath my leaking cock. I thrust my own against it, collecting some of the lube from the motion as more tips and comments came flooding in.

Leaning back on my bed, I spread my legs, positioning myself front and center so my audience could watch me fuck my fingers one at a time. Because I didn't do this often, I knew I needed to work myself up, which meant the video would be longer than my usual ten minutes, but I supposed once in a while a little variety was good, right?

My cock *ached*, throbbing with need as I slid my fingers out, positioning the giant cock at my wet, lubricated entrance. The tingling pressure as I inched the silicone shaft in was maddening, and I wanted to come almost immediately. I caught my breath, my eyes falling closed as I stretched myself to capacity.

Ungh.

So fucking full.

With a shaky hand, I let go, my balls and cock aching for release. I righted myself, going to my knees once more, which made the toy shoved in my ass bottom out completely. Letting out a slow breath, I carefully bent over in the slightest motion, rocking my hips against it, grabbing my slick cock with my free hand. With every thrust into my warm, wet hands, the dildo slid out of me just a hair. Back and forth, I built a slow, torturous rhythm.

In my brain, I imagined it was him.

Bending me over his desk, fucking me because once again I was *his* dirty little whore.

I needed to be punished by him, I needed to be *good.*

I came with a force that was unexpected, but welcome. I closed my eyes as I rode the wave of my orgasm, my insides contracting around the foreign invader as I continued the onslaught of my release, my stomach muscles and abs contracting with each pulse. For a moment, I felt like anything was possible.

With my eyes closed, I could pretend it was him fucking me into oblivion, wrapping those long arms and legs around me.

Holding me as he unloaded himself inside me, making me his.

But when I opened my eyes to see I'd

cum not just all over myself, but on the bed, the incessant ringing of tips and comments, I felt a deeper ache than anything else I'd ever felt.

Because as good as I felt—and I felt *amazing*—I felt a wave of guilt that what I desired. What I wanted more than anything would never come to fruition. I felt *guilty.* Not just about what I'd done, but about who I was.

I wanted more than the emptiness I felt at that moment.

All the comments and the tips in the world would never feel as good as his kiss.

As his touch.

Nothing.

And so I wiped my sticky, cum-filled hand on my leg, dismounted my silicone friend, and turned off the camera. Tears threatened to break free, but I bit my tongue, stifling them down.

I'd just cleaned up my space when I saw the comments still flooding in on my phone. I almost pushed the thing away, but I didn't. Because one notification stood out among the rest.

A text message.

Are you busy Friday night?

Naked, I stood there, staring at a text message for the second time that day, only this one was more chilling, more frightening than a brunch invite.

Because every bone in my body wanted to say *yes.*

For you, I could be free even during an apocalypse.

I answered with a cool, *Yeah. Why, you want a rematch at that air hockey game?*

Best to sound nonchalant. I wouldn't want Sunday Best to get the wrong idea and think I'm just waiting on pins and needles for his call.

Even though that's exactly what I'd been doing.

Tempting, but... my brother and some of his friends and I are going to check out some clubs for the Bachelor party location. Was wondering if you wanted to be my plus one?

I knew better than most that the arcade wasn't actually a date, despite how much it felt like it was. It was just hanging out.

But this, deliberately asking me to join him and his family, a group of his friends, clubbing...

Friends are a big deal. It most certainly felt like a date.

I knew I should put an end to what was happening between us, what was happening to me, because every time I wound up around the man, I got soft. My walls started to crumble, and I dared to dream, to hope maybe this time could be different, even though I knew it wouldn't' be. That was, if I told him the truth.

But I was a fool for Mr. Riley Evans, it seemed. And I didn't want to do the right thing.

I wanted to do very, very bad things. To him...

Yeah, that sounds fun. Where should I meet you?

I sat on the edge of my bed, the cool air of my bedroom contrasting with the fire in my blood, in my being, as I waited for his answer.

I'll pick you up around eight thirty.

After sending a thumbs up, I fell back on my bed, staring at the ceiling as the ominous truth loomed over me.

I knew what I needed to do, but perhaps there was nothing wrong with having a little fun first, right?

CHAPTER SEVENTEEN

Riley

IT'S NOT A date.

Though my sweaty palms, flippant stomach, and nerves begged to differ.

I couldn't remember the last time I'd agonized this much over what to wear to an event that wasn't a fundraiser or a funeral.

The school was pretty laid back when it came to our attire, so most of the time I just wore my chinos and a polo to keep things comfortable and simple, and when I was home it was sweatpants and old t-shirts.

At the risk of my 'not getting properly

laid', Chris had taken it upon himself to chaperone me after school on my trip to Kohls to make sure I was 'thirst trap material.'

For a straight man, I had to admit, he did have a keen eye for fashion.

I'd settled on a shimmery chrome-like shirt that changed color with the light. The sleeves stopped at my elbow, to give the illusion of a rolled up sleeve, but really they were just cut that way.

Chris even talked me into getting a pair of black jeans to pair with the shirt. Jeans he said would really accentuate my *assets*, whatever that meant.

"Now, I expect a full report on Monday, and I don't want to hear none of that holding hands bullshit. You have one mission this weekend—"

"To find a location for my brother's bachelor party?" I drawled as I finished wiping down the blackboard.

"To get fucking laid," Chris said, miming a basketball shot into an imaginary hoop.

"Shhh. The kids are still here..."

Chris rolled his eyes. "Trust me, my foul mouth is not the worst thing these kids have heard on a Friday after school," he said with a laugh. "Don't change the subject. What's your mission?"

I sighed, knowing it was best to just go along with his antics. But also I supposed, given the fact he'd insisted on helping me at all, it was the least I could do.

"My mission is to have *fun* and..." I sighed, first checking to make sure no one else was in earshot before I breathed out, "Get laid."

Chris bit his knuckle, feigning a mother hen's look of approval. "God, they grow up so fast."

I rolled my eyes as I grabbed my blazer, heading for the door.

"Have fun on your date!" he hollered so loud I worried the damn office would hear. Even though they were more than a ten minute walk away.

"It's not a date!" I yelled back as I turned the corner, grinning ear to ear.

Date or no date, I meant what I'd said. Tonight was about having fun, and as far as I was concerned, that was my mission.

To drink, dance, and have fun with Eric, my brother, and our friends.

CHAPTER EIGHTEEN

Riley

I PULLED UP to Eric's house at eight twenty on the nose. With the hurricane in my stomach still swirling, and the sweat starting to bead on my trim chest beneath the hot fabric of my shirt, I knew it was now or never. Just as I opened my phone to text him, I heard the door close.

I glanced up through my windshield to see Eric standing there in a pair of *leather* pants, with a hot pink shirt. With the sleeves rolled up to his elbow, nice and tight. His clothes were perfectly fitted to his form, showcasing his natural shape.

In my headlights, his skin looked pale, his eyes bright like sapphires, dark hair falling in his eyes like some cross between John Stamos in his Uncle Jesse era and Ian Somerhalder in his Vampire Diaries era.

He was so fucking *hot,* and my cock more than agreed.

I barely noticed when he opened the door on his own, silently chastising myself that I should have just shut my mouth and met him on the porch, walked him to the car.

"I was going to text you," I said, like a dumbass.

"You're early," he said, licking his lips.

"You were waiting," I said, as I realized at that moment he'd been more than ready. I'd barely been in his driveway long enough to text, and he was out, locked up, and in my car.

He was *waiting* for me.

Like a date.

"I like to be on time, sue me." He shrugged, dismissing my comment. His tone was flirtatious, causing a smile to form on my lips as I waited until he'd put his seatbelt on before backing up.

The sounds of Miguel's *Sure Thing* graced the speakers, the smooth beats somewhat relaxing.

"No smutty audiobooks on our ride today?" Eric taunted.

Though the way he spoke, his voice was better than any audio narrator I'd ever heard.

"Oh, I'm done with that one," I said.

Eric relaxed in his seat, and I could feel his eyes on me. Like he was sizing me up or something, as the singer swooned on about being the reporter and the news.

"Too bad, I was hoping maybe I would get to see you all flustered by dirty words again," he said, leaning his arm along the window frame. "You, uh, you're kinda cute when you're all flustered."

His compliment went straight to my cock, then back up to my brain, making my cheeks redden along the way.

Did he just call me cute?

Then his tone softened as he shifted in his seat.

"Um, thanks, I think," I said, letting out a chuckle. I could feel his gaze on me, hot like fire.

"You know, you don't have to, like, be embarrassed about that shit. What you like is, what you like, you know? You don't have to feel weird about it. I just wanted to say that."

Truth was, I loved to read romance, but I'd never considered the things I read in my books as preferences or anything. Not that I had many people to test the waters with, anyway.

But something about Eric's words made me feel like maybe it was okay to be open about my preferences.

My desires.

Desires that might include him starring in my own personal show.

Maybe reading to me and then...

My cock stiffened at the thought, and I let out a sigh as I admitted to him, "I'm just not used to sharing my preferences or my taste in literature with other people." I swallowed harshly. "Especially other men.."

Yeah, men who I imagine taking the place of said fictional characters.

"You know there's, like, a wild ass community of people who are into smutty books, right?" he said seriously.

"Yeah, but how many guys do you

know actually *listen* to gay romance?"

Eric's eyes sparkled for a moment as he smiled. "I think you'd be surprised."

His tone made me feel at ease, which was truly dangerous. Being around Eric, it was just so easy to be myself.

To talk, to play.

So, I didn't think twice before word vomiting out, "Are you? Into gay romance novels, I mean?"

Eric laughed, and I loved the sound.

That first night I'd seen him in the bar, playing pool, I'd assumed he was just a cocky asshole who didn't like to lose. Who thought he was all that and a bag of chips.

But in the days since then, I'd come to learn that while he most certainly did not like to lose, he wasn't some cocky asshole that was full of himself. If anything, I thought his cocky attitude was a front for covering up the person he really was, and that was something I could relate to. I wore a mask too.

Eric was funny, and easy to talk to. He was attractive, and mysterious, and I really liked being around him. I liked who *I* was around him.

Unapologetic.

Free.

Could this... could this serendipitous thing be something more?

More than just friends or a plus one type situation?

I dared to wonder what that would be like.

A lot of fucking fun, probably.

Eric shifted in his seat, propping his knee up as he got comfortable.

"Um, not quite novels, but I'm well versed in smut, you could say," he said, his voice dropping an octave to sound even *better* than my audio narrator.

Maybe he should be narrating audiobooks...

Well versed in smut.

The words alone made my cock twitch and my heart jump.

I was so out of my league.

"Well, good," I said, swallowing harshly. "Because I'm fairly certain I'm going to need your help tonight."

"For the bachelor party, you mean?" he asked.

I nodded. "It's kind of this unspoken thing between my brother and the other party members. They all think..." I started.

"They all think what?" Eric asked curiously.

The words were on the tip of my tongue. I knew what I wanted to say, but somehow saying it out loud made it a thousand times worse.

I looked at Eric, at his pristine blue eyes that coaxed me like a lamb to slaughter.

No embarrassment, no judgment.

"I know they think I'm going to make it lame. Like I don't know what's sexy, or what, you know, most guys are into."

Eric raised an eyebrow, in surprise. "How so?"

I looked at him as I huffed a sigh of annoyance.

Might as well just get it off my chest before I see everyone tonight.

"Because everyone thinks I'm some goody two shoes who can't let loose and have fucking fun." I sighed, as the words continued, flowing free of their own accord.

"And because I'm gay, like, they think I can't pick out good strippers or something. Hell if I know."

Eric laughed, and the sound was deep and sexy. It was infectious, and I couldn't help but laugh too.

Being with Eric was like that. Somehow, he found a way to infiltrate my fortresses and remind me who I was underneath it all.

Who I'd *forgotten* I was.

"But you're not, are you?" he asked inquisitively. "You're not the person everyone thinks you are."

"I mean, I'm gay, but I'm not blind," I bit out.

Eric chuckled once more.

My brother wouldn't come out and say such things, and I knew the other members of the party were not as organized, and no one was jumping at the bit to volunteer as tribute to plan a night of debauchery, but I could read between the lines.

I was fully intent on giving my brother the best bachelor party I could, because he deserved it. Even it meant I had to stomach a night of tits and ass that did not appeal to me.

It had to be perfect, and I knew between him, our friends, and Eric, I'd manage to make it the best.

"Is that why you invited me, Riley? To help you pick out strippers?" Eric chuckled.

The conversation was steering off the beaten path while I focused on the GPS telling me to turn onto Rodal Road, which meant we'd be at *Cheerleaders* in no time.

"I mean, can you blame me for wanting to bring along some personal eye candy?" I teased him.

Though his voice changed from playful, almost to sad.

"No, guess I can't."

A strange sort of tension fell between us, but I had no time to dwell on such things. I parked the car, just as my phone was ringing. It was my brother.

I opened the car door, sprinting around to get Eric's. His gaze met mine as I nodded with a smile, telling my brother we were there.

And when I finished up with him on the phone, I offered Eric my arm. I watched as he contemplated taking it, almost as if he were afraid.

"Are you ready to meet the rest of the party and have some fun?" I asked, my nerves starting to settle.

Eric flashed me a smile that made my stomach flip. "I thought you'd never ask."

CHAPTER NINETEEN

Riley

THANKFULLY, THE CLUB district packed their buildings close together, and therefore we could easily hop from one place to the next. Our first stop of the night was *Cheerleaders*, and though I'd never stepped foot in a straight strip club before, I could see the appeal.

My brother and Eric toasted their shot glasses as the rest of the party, Lane, Grayson, Henry, and even Drew Axel—Giselle's rockstar buddy—and his boyfriend—the florist, Taylor—had come out for the event, and all were lined up at the bar, "testing" out the shots amid a myriad of fans who were taking selfies and getting their boobs signed by Drew.

"What are you waiting for? Christmas?" Grayson said as he came up beside me, holding out a shot.

I sniffed the concoction. It smelled like pumpkin-scented glass cleaner.

"What the hell is this, anyway?" I asked. I'd had two beers, which gave me an okay buzz, but I wasn't planning on getting drunk at the first place we checked out. I wanted to take note, observe the place and Aaron's reactions. Plus, shots weren't really my thing, but that was what everyone seemed to gravitate toward there.

Grayson smirked, and I could see the resemblance to his sister. They both had the same look of mischief.

"It's called a Pumpkinhead. Tastes like pumpkin pie."

"Gross," I said, as Grayson laughed.

"It's not so bad if you chuck it really fast," he teased.

"Yeah, that's the point, right? Fastest way to drunk is with a bunch of shots."

Grayson shrugged as he shot his in one swift motion, offering me the other.

"I prefer to get shitfaced on an

exquisitely aged cab, but alas, straight men have the worst taste in drinks, I'm afraid."

I couldn't help but let out a chuckle as I shook my head. Thankfully, I wasn't the only gay man at the strip club tonight. Though Grayson, Henry, Drew, and Taylor looked far more comfortable with all the beautiful women surrounding our party than I felt at the moment. Even surrounded by the sights and sounds, they didn't seem to notice much more than their significant others.

In fact, as I surveyed the bar, I could see Drew and Taylor grinding on one another with smiles plastered all over their faces like lovesick teenagers.

I wished it were that easy for me. That I could have an ounce of sex appeal like Drew Axel, or the confidence of Grayson.

I took the shot from his hands, but my gaze was set on something else. Someone else. The object of my turmoil.

Ever since our car ride, something was different. I couldn't put my finger on it, but whatever it was, was driving me crazy. All I wanted to do was give the guy a hug and tell him I was sorry, for whatever it was I did, because clearly I was an idiot, and I'd done *something.*

I watched as Eric and my brother toasted another round of shots. I thought it was the third one.

Eric seemed to get along with my brother swimmingly. Granted, they'd met before, but we'd all been far too preoccupied with our game to properly make each other's acquaintances or get to know one another.

I watched as a woman in shorts and a bikini top sauntered over to my brother, squeezing between him and Eric.

She threw her arms around Eric, making a kissy face as she took a selfie with him. Though I couldn't blame her. In his hot pink shirt, tight black jeans, with his gorgeous face and the charisma that just rolled off of him every time he walked into a room.

"You know you are allowed to have fun too," Grayson said softly.

"I am having fun," I grumbled as I downed my shot.

Grayson twisted his lips. "Aaron is having fun. Your little boyfriend is having fun. You... you are *watching.* You're stalling."

I shot Grayson a raised eyebrow of my own. "For starters, Aaron is the one who should be having fun because this is about *him*. About the perfect bachelor party," I said with a sigh. "And Eric is *not* my boyfriend. I'm observing, you know, to take in the *ambiance* for scientific purposes," I drawled sarcastically.

Grayson shook his head, raising an eyebrow. "Really? I mean, you brought him, so I assumed..."

My gaze settled on Eric's bright smile as Aaron laughed at something he said.

"Plus, you've been staring at him for like ten minutes."

Grayson's words settled on me, stirring the hurricane inside of me again.

Had I really been staring that long?

Before I could say anything, Grayson's tone shifted. "Shit or get off the pot, Riley. Because if you don't make your move, I guarantee you someone else will."

I turned to him, raising my eyes. "Excuse me?" I said.

Grayson gestured with his gaze to the woman who was now *grinding* on Eric, bending over to twerk her ass against his crotch, her mouth at Aaron's waist level. Lane hooted and hollered as I watched Eric settle his hand on her jean-clad ass, and my blood boiled.

I realized as I meant to speak, I didn't know that Eric *wasn't* into women. Not every guy who liked dick hated pussy. Some preferred both.

Panic flooded me along with doubt. I'd been so focused on my own embarrassment, during our *preferences* conversation, it occurred to me I never asked if he had any preferences of his own.

Because I was nervous, and asking such things felt too intimate for friends.

But as the word settled in my brain—friends—I realized I didn't like the sound of it.

I didn't want to be *friends* with Eric.

I liked him. I liked him a whole hell of a lot, and as the realization struck me, I felt the air around me get thinner.

My gaze fixed on him as he danced with her, laughing with her, and I couldn't help but feel the pang of desire to be her.

To be the one held under his captivating gaze, to feel his hand on *my ass*, fingers grabbing *my* hips.

While I stuffed his mouth full of my cock.

My cock twitched at the thought, my heart beating faster with jealousy and desire, and I realized I wanted to know everything there was to know about Eric. I wanted to be the object of *his* desire. This wasn't about finding a date to my brother's wedding.

Not anymore.

I wanted to spend as much time as I could with the man who made me feel like I'd finally awakened from a long sleep.

But for all the strides I'd made, I was still sitting in the damn dugout, watching the game be played. Because I was scared.

I was scared that if I pushed too hard, Eric would run away.

Needy.

Desperate.

Stage five clinger.

The words my exes labeled me with rolled around in my brain.

How had things become so complicated?

Why couldn't I just walk over there,

tell him how I felt, kiss him, and take him home?

I watched as Eric bent down, hands behind his back and sucked a shot from between her breasts, liquor running down his chin as Aaron fist bumped the air, the rest of the men at the bar cheering him on. He grabbed the shot glass from his mouth, slamming it down on the bar as everyone cheered. Aaron high-fived him. Watching him with my brother and the party, he fit in perfectly.

Like he *belonged* with them.

A fresh wave of jealousy rolled through me. Grayson's voice pulled me from my trance, and I realized he was still standing there beside me. Watching, observing.

"He's a pretty fish, but so are you. You're an Evans, for Christ sake. Own that shit. Stop staring and second-guessing yourself, and get the fuck over there. Blow his fucking mind. Make him forget everyone else," Grayson said, clapping me on the back. "That's what I did, and it worked for me." Grayson grinned before he headed toward Henry, who wrapped his arms around his boyfriend the moment he stepped into his proximity at the bar.

At that moment, I caught Eric's sapphire gaze, noting how the corners of his lips turned up in a smirk. Like he was truly *baiting* me.

And perhaps it was the shot, or the neon lights that danced over him, or the rage of jealousy, or Grayson's pep talk, but whatever it was, was enough.

Grayson was right. I wasn't a clam hiding under the mud, not anymore.

I was an *Evans.*

My brother may have been the sporty, pretty jock, but I was not without my charms. I could be commanding, and hot, and... and...

I found myself pulled into Eric's orbit once more as I slid between him and the pretty little tart who was downing another shot, this time with my brother and Lane.

The sounds of *Dirty Dancer* by Usher and Enrique came over the speakers, and in the distance, I could see a topless woman flipping herself upside down at the top of her pole, which was the only pole in the room to go from high vaulted ceiling to floor.

Okay, that's pretty impressive, to be

honest.

"Having fun yet, Professorrr?" Eric said, slightly slurring his r's as he slammed down his shot glass.

"Not quite. Standing around doing shots isn't my idea of fun," I said as I slid the shot glass toward the barkeep, shaking my head to say we were done for the moment.

Aaron and Lane were laughing about something as one of the strippers tugged and pulled at Drew, begging him to take the stage with them.

Eric extended his arms along the bar, the motion drawing attention to his defined forearms. He blew some dark hair out of his eyes, with his pouty, perfect lips. He leaned back, crossing his legs, enticing me apathetically with his perfect pout, his bright blue eyes, and his flirtatious, sensual look.

His tone was cheerful, but his eyes didn't sparkle like they usually did.

"Awww, is the victor not enjoying his spoils?" Eric taunted, the alcohol making him sound huskier than usual.

"I'd enjoy it a lot more if I could pry you away from the bar... and handsy strippers," I said as my brother and his cohorts hooted and hollered yet again, chasing the pretty girl who was all over Eric moments ago, and Drew toward the stage.

"Oh, is that what you want..." Eric said, slowly taking a step toward me, his blue gaze full of sadness, despite the grin on his face. His dark hair fell in his face, and instinctively, I pushed it away, behind the shell of his ear.

"You want to whisk me away in your carriage off to your fucking castle, Cinderella?" he breathed out.

I settled my hand on his hips, captivated by his gaze, his hot breath on my skin.

"Like you're my knight in shining armor?"

"There are a lot of things I want to do with you," I whispered, letting my thumb trace his solid jawline.

Eric looked up at me, his gaze imploring mine. "Green's a good color on you, Riley," Eric purred, his fingers teasing the loops of my jeans.

"I'm not jealous," I huffed as the bartender slid me a shot. "I said—"

"This one's from the guy down there," he said, nodding to Grayson, who held up a shot, Henry wrapped around him like a coiled snake.

I took the shot, pursing my lips. After all, I didn't want to be impolite. I raised it, shot it, and slammed it back down on the bar. The burn of the pumpkin-flavored vanilla liquor was prevalent, and I sucked in a deep breath.

"I'm just testing out the product. Isn't that what you brought me here for?" Eric's breath against my neck was warm, and I leaned closer into him, his fingertips trailing lightly over my thigh, just next to my aching cock.

I stared down at him with a mixture of fury and desire, of jealousy and arousal. I wanted to kiss him. In this stupid room full of pert breasts and clapping cheeks, underneath the neon lights.

But I wanted *more* too.

I wanted to explore Eric's mysterious alleyways until I knew every corner and crevice of his mind, body, and soul.

"Dance with me," I breathed, my heart thudding loudly in my chest. It wasn't a request.

It was a *need*.

I needed to feel Eric's body pressed

against me, needed to feel his lips on mine, his hardness against mine. The desire was overwhelming, especially this close, knowing we weren't truly alone.

Eric snickered, showcasing his pearly white canines in a way that was so undeniably *hot* it made me wonder if I had a fetish for sexy grins.

Or perhaps just a fetish for pretty boys with attitudes.

"Careful, Riley. You're starting to sound like a possessive asshole. All demanding and shit," Eric teased.

My cock stiffened in my tight pants, and a part of me worried someone— anyone—would see the burgeoning tent forming.

Seriously, how do guys wear pants this tight?

But as I looked into Eric's pristine eyes, as the sounds of Enrique crooned about never being lonely, for the first time, I didn't care.

I *wanted* someone to see us. To see me with my hands on his hips, my lips on his.

Mine, mine, mine.

"I thought you weren't into strippers," I said, my voice dark and gravelly as he smirked back at me.

"Awww, is that what has your panties in a twist? Worried I'll trade you in for some pussy?" he drawled brattily.

The overwhelming desire to turn him around, bend him over the closest bar stool, and make him eat his words was a new feeling for me.

I wanted to erase anyone and everyone else from his mind, just like Grayson suggested.

"Careful, *Eric*, you're starting to sound like a petulant little cock tease," I said the words without thinking, emboldened by his behavior, the shots, and his gorgeous face.

The club music died out, and in it's place I heard Drew Axel crooning some rock version of Taylor Swift song.

Which one I had no clue, but the words resonated with me nonetheless.

I settled my hand on Eric's hip, gently tugging him closer. This close, his body against mine was warm, and I could feel the faint twitch of his cock against me.

Did he like this?

My own cock throbbed in response as I breathed him in, like he was oxygen.

As nervous as I was, it felt *good*.

Like I was breaking a barrier, jumping off a cliff.

Eric rolled his eyes, a dark chuckle escaping his throat.

"Let's get one thing straight here, Princess," he said as he walked his fingers up the buttons on my shirt, stopping as he grabbed me by my collar, yanking me *down* to his eye level.

His eyes burned like fire, and while a part of me was shocked at the touch, the *strength* and the force...

The rest of me was turned the hell *on*.

Fucking hell... This man...

"I am no cock tease. When I want something, I take it." His words were clear, not a slur to be heard in them.

He loosened his grip just the slightest, his fingertips brushing against my skin. At this level, his lips were inches away, ripe for the taking.

I didn't think twice. I only acted on impulse, on selfish need.

He didn't startle or jump, or try and push me away.

Instead, his fingers slid up my neck, into the edges of my hair at the nape of my neck, seeking purchase there. He let me take his kiss like a damn robbery, and that was where I realized I was drowning.

Eric wasn't just a pretty fish.

He was an elusive shark, and I was falling in love with him, hook, line, and sinker.

CHAPTER TWENTY

Riley

I LEANED AGAINST the leather couch in *Pleasure Dome,* the newest club on the block, which I'd heard was a bit more risqué than the others. Though there were at least four conjoined clubs on the strip here, we'd only made it to two.

The room was spinning, but I couldn't deny I didn't feel *good.*

Drew Axel fell beside me as I blinked, the neon lights blurring my vision.

I couldn't remember the last time I'd been this shitfaced.

Probably college.

"I booked us all a block at the

Renaissance across the street," Drew said, his voice much clearer than anyone else in our party.

"What?" I asked, trying to make sense of my surroundings. My gaze settled on Eric, who was on the dance floor, dancing on his own in the middle of the crowd. Aaron, Lane, Henry, Grayson, and Taylor were all strewn about the floor and bar. I had no idea what time it was, but the place was still thick with patrons, and strippers dressed in tight black latex outfits that were strategically cut out in all the right places.

"Tell them you're with Drew Axel. They'll hook you two up with a room."

I looked at him for a moment, his face slightly doubled.

"I'm so fucking drunk right now," I said, not giving a shit if I sounded like an idiot.

Drew laughed, shaking his head.

"I know, buddy. You're not the only one." He chuckled, clapping me on the shoulder.

"You?" I asked.

Drew shook his head as Taylor came to sit next to him.

"Not me. I'm the DD," he said as

Taylor kissed him, stealing his attention for a moment. "Though I gotta say, your brother made it seem like you'd be the responsible one," he said with a laugh, wrapping his arm around his boyfriend. "But even the good guys need to go a little bad sometimes. Right, baby?" he cooed, placing a quick kiss on his boyfriend's lips.

Seeing them so comfortable with one another, so *in love*, made me jealous. But it also made me hopeful.

"I am re... re.. responsa-bb-le." I tried to say the words, but my wires were crossed, and it came out rather unintelligent.

Eric sauntered over toward us, his dark hair slick from the sweat of dancing as he leaned over, extending a hand to help me up.

"Drew says we should go hotel," I said, trying to make sense of my words.

"What?" Eric said. The music was loud, so I yelled what I'd said.

"Renaissance. Front desk, tell them Drew Axel Party," Drew's words echoed around us as I let Eric pull me off the leather couch. I stumbled into his arms, nearly knocking him over, but he held me steady.

My legs felt like Jell-O, and he smelled like sweat, liquor, and cedar cologne.

He smelled like pure sex, and my cock more than agreed.

"Yeah, okay," Eric said as he wrapped his arm around my waist. I liked how it felt there. "Probably not a bad idea…"

I leaned down, placing a kiss on his neck, like Taylor had done only moments ago to his boyfriend.

Boyfriend…

Eric grunted a sound that went straight to my cock, my hands trailing over his chest. The thumping bass of the club echoed with my heartbeat, and I ground my cock against him.

"Uber's here," Eric said, his voice deep, gravelly.

"Okay," I whispered huskily as he steadied me.

"We'll walk you out," Drew said, leading the way.

The lights, the sounds, all of it was dizzying as we made our way through the crowds, outside to the black SUV waiting for us. Eric and I tumbled in the backseat as Drew closed the door.

My lips were on Eric's in a matter of seconds as I pulled him closer, into my lap. His kiss was wet and loose as his lips traveled over mine, along my jaw. My cock throbbed in my tight pants, and the need to take off my jeans and briefs was overwhelming.

"We're here," Eric slurred as the car came to a stop.

The door opened, and the cool air kissed my skin. Eric's fingers slid into mine as we walked into the bright lit lobby. I followed Eric to the desk, letting him lead.

It felt good to have someone else in charge for once.

"Drew Axel... Party," he said, his tone sounding much more crisp and clear than mine.

I watched as my vision sharpened slightly, as the woman presented us a card with a gold-embossed number seventeen.

Eric grabbed it with his free hand, never letting mine go.

I squeezed his hand, liking the feel of his warm palm against my own.

We wandered through the first floor, and thankfully, the room was close.

Though it took a few tries to get the scanner to click, once it did, all bets were off.

No sooner than the door was locked was I unfastening my belt, angling to set my restrained cock free.

My back smacked against the wall as Eric's hands took over, his lips at my neck, biting, sucking.

"Fucking hell, I'm so hard," I murmured, the words falling out of my mouth without warning.

"Me too," Eric purred, his fingers sliding down my pants. I fumbled for his, my fingers making steady work of finding his buttons, and instead, my hand roved over his hardness, squeezing him through his jeans.

"Who's the cock tease, now?" he grumbled, thrusting himself against my palm.

I unbuttoned his leather pants, shoving them down with his underwear in one fell swoop.

I settled my hands on his warm, sweaty hips, over his ass, as I pulled him against me. His thick length against mine had me seeing stars, and I couldn't help the moan that left my mouth at the feel of precum sliding along my shaft.

Though I wasn't sure if it was mine or his...

"Fuck, Eric..." I closed my eyes as I wrapped my hand around our slick cocks, needing more. I slowly built a rhythm, pumping us both.

Eric leaned his head against my chest, his fingers working the buttons of my shirt as he thrust himself against me.

"I want you," I breathed.

"Oh, yeah?" he drawled, busting open my shirt, taking my nipple in his mouth. His teeth grazed the sensitive skin, making me cry out as a fresh blossom of precum coated me.

"How do you want me, *Professor?*" His voice was dark, full of things that made my stomach turn in knots, made my cock throb.

"I want..." I found it hard to think, let alone breathe as Eric laved his tongue across my chest, wrapping his mouth around my other nipple as I pumped our cocks slowly.

"I want *Daddy* to get on his knees," I purred, seeking his mouth with mine. His kiss was a rush of heat and he tasted like heaven.

I wanted to drown in his kiss, his touch.

Underneath him, I felt *alive.*

"So demanding," Eric touted as I let go of our cocks.

I made haste of unbuttoning his shirt, letting my hands explore his solid, hard chest.

In my hazy vision, he was a sight for sore eyes. Lips swollen from kissing me, blue eyes ablaze with lust, hair slicked back from sweat and heat.

I watched as he grabbed himself, running his thumb over his leaking cock.

"What will you do for me?" he breathed, and I couldn't help licking my lips.

Standing before me, naked, he was like a living wet dream.

I wanted everything.

Everything this perfect man was willing to give me.

"Whatever you want, *Daddy,*" I uttered. "I'm yours for the taking."

Eric pulled me from against the wall, leading me back through the room, and I followed him without hesitation. His lips caressed mine again as he pushed me down onto the bed. He nudged my legs open, and I leaned up on my elbows to look at him where he stood.

His cock gleamed in the bedroom light. He stood between my legs, gazing down at me as he *spit* directly onto my cock, making it throb once more. His gaze held mine as he slathered my cock in his saliva, breathing heavily.

"Whatever I want, huh?" he whispered, his voice dark and gravelly and filled with heat.

I nodded in response, my heart racing, waiting for his kiss, his touch, his mouth.

I needed release.

"Yes, yes... please..."

"Please, what?" he purred, dropping to his knees, licking me from base to tip slowly.

I arched my back, thrusting my cock at him, but he relented, teasing, taunting me.

"Please, Eric..." His name on my tongue was a mixture of pleasure, of pain, and of hope.

Please put me out of my misery, once and for all.

Eric's fingers dug into my ass cheeks as he *yanked* me off the bed, taking my cock into the back of his throat.

I took him into the back of my throat in one fell swoop until I couldn't breathe, his deep groan only making my own cock throb even more as he grabbed me by the back of my hair.

The words from my audiobook echoed in my drunken brain.

Eric groaned as he sucked me, fingers squeezing my flesh as my legs stiffened around his head.

"Oh fuck..." I could feel my orgasm on the edge, so close, yet so far away.

I sat up the best I could, but my upper half felt like Jell-O, and my lower half was hot, buzzing with anticipation as Eric licked and sucked me, hollowing his cheeks like I was a damn tootsie roll pop and his mission was discover how many licks it took to find the center.

"Eric..." I cried out, knowing I wasn't going to last.

I reached out, sliding my hand into his hair. I wanted to grab him, but I had no strength, no concentration. Everything pooled to my balls, my cock. I fought to lift my hips, to fuck his mouth like I had imagined when I thought of him in the confines of my shower.

But my grip was weak and my entire body shuddered as I came. I cried out in ecstasy, my words jumbling into an array of his name and some cursing. He didn't let go of me as my grip loosened in his hair, sucking down every bit of me until I was empty.

My legs and body were tingling with numbness like I was made of nothing but pure magic.

His cock slid against mine as he righted me, straddling my chest.

I looked up at him, dazed, watching as he held his thick, swollen cock above me.

"Open wide for Daddy, Professor," he commanded.

And I did.

I obeyed him without second thought.

I opened my mouth, watching as he threw his head back, pumping his shaft above me, fucking my mouth with rapid, heated thrusts, and within seconds, he erupted.

Though I would be remiss to say his aim was not the best, and neither was mine. He came on my chest, my face, and only partly in my mouth, but I didn't care.

Eric cursed as he fell back onto the bed beside me, the only sound our deep breaths, and contentment.

I curled next to him, throwing a hand over his hip as I fell into deep slumber, and I dreamed of wet, sloppy kisses and audiobooks, and dancing under the stars with the man of my dreams.

CHAPTER TWENTY-ONE

Eric

MY HEAD WAS pounding, and I was sweltering beneath the sheets. Sheets that didn't feel like my own thousand thread count Egyptian cotton.

I blinked, my eyes adjusting to the bright light as I shielded myself from it. Once my vision sharpened, I realized I was certainly *not* at home.

And I was most certainly *naked.*

Fuck!

Before I could process my surroundings or how I'd ended up in a bed I didn't know, I heard the door open. I turned to see Riley, standing there in nothing but a white towel—his trim chest on display, the pale skin speckled with sparse, dark hair that swiftly led down his abdomen beneath the towel. Freshly showered dark hair hung in his eyes messily and panic spread within me.

I racked my brain, but I could not remember *anything* past Cheerleaders. I was drawing a literal blank at the moment.

Oh my God, did we—

"You're up," Riley said, as he took a slow step toward me.

My heart was running rampant as I tried to piece everything together, and I tried to remember just how badly I'd fucked up.

This is not how this was supposed to happen!

This was not supposed to happen at all!

"I'm so sorry…" I said, running a hand through my hair as shame and guilt built within me.

Riley stood before me, the fresh scent of hotel shampoo and body wash wafting off of him. My stomach flipped as I stared at the sight of him, looming over me, looking like absolute perfection at this hour. My cock twitched in response, and I felt as if I could barely breathe under his gaze.

"I'm not," he said, his voice soft, even.

His words washed over me, and I couldn't help but close my eyes, soaking them in.

God, I wished I could remember what happened.

"I don't... I must have blacked out. I... I don't remember what happened past Cheerleaders," I admitted, feeling embarrassed.

I couldn't remember the last time I legit blacked out. I usually liked to be in control of myself and the situation.

When I opened my eyes, I saw Riley's furrowed eyebrows as he took a seat beside me on the bed. The bed squeaked a little, and a fresh pounding assaulted my head, and I felt a bit uneasy.

"Is that what's bothering you?" he asked, his voice barely a whisper.

"I mean, this isn't my first rodeo, but..." I said, not wanting to sound like a whiny little bitch or something. Lord knew I'd had my share of scenarios just like this, only I was the one being regretted.

Did I regret what happened?

I wasn't so sure... and that only made my insides twist some more.

I pulled my knees up to my chest beneath the covers.

How had things gotten so complicated?

"How did we even get here?" I asked, running a hand over my face.

"Apparently Drew Axel reserved a block of rooms for us, due to our... festivities going a bit overboard. He texted me just before I jumped in the shower. Checking to make sure we'd gotten in all right."

I dared to steal a glance at Riley, not wanting to ask but needing to know all the same.

"I, uh, don't normally do this sort of thing, you know."

I scoffed, refusing to look at him for the moment. I didn't want to see regret or pity in his eyes.

"What sort of thing?" I grumbled.

"Take attractive men home. I mean, I know this isn't home or anything..." he said hurriedly. I glanced at him from beneath my lashes.

"I usually don't drink so much either… I'm usually the responsible one, you know?" he asked, sighing.

The need, the desire to make him feel better, even when I was struggling for sanity myself was overwhelming.

"Do you remember what happened?" I asked.

Riley's gaze softened. "Bits and pieces, yes."

I attempted to soothe his own crisis at the moment, assuring him this wasn't what I usually did either.

Except, if I was being honest… I did do this sort of thing. Not often, but…

I didn't usually do it with people I had feelings for.

Did I have feelings for Riley?

I wanted to say no, but the truth was so much more complicated than that.

"I didn't mean to take advantage, of you I mean, I…" I breathed out a sigh as panic laced me. "I don't even know if you're…"

It was a stupid thing to say, to imply that I was panicking about whether or not Riley was clean, and it was even dumber to insist that was what was bothering me when I knew the truth.

While I'd hooked up with guys via dating apps a couple times, I never performed with anyone, and I had a record that was spotless. I would have bet a million dollars Mr. Sunday Best was cleaner than a whistle.

Riley's shoulders fell, his lips pursed as he ran a hand through his hair.

"Oh my God, I didn't even think..."

"I'm clean," I blurted out, quickly hurrying through my confession if only to put it out in the open if it would help soothe Riley's nerves a fraction.

Hell, maybe it will even soothe my own.

"I mean, in case you, uh, were worried," I said, like an idiot.

"I mean, we probably should have had this discussion before we..." I watched as his cheeks reddened.

"Fucked?" I asked hesitantly, the question hanging in the air.

My heart raced as I bit my lip, waiting for his confirmation.

"Actually, all I remember is you, um, on your knees..." he said, quickly recovering with, "And then I remember returning the favor, and then... I think we fell asleep because I had some weird dreams. We didn't, um, fuck," he said, and despite the redness in his cheeks, I couldn't deny the word on his tongue made my cock twitch.

A part of me was relieved, but also disappointed. Though there was no doubt in the world I wanted to drive the fine specimen next to me into next Tuesday with my cock, and I certainly wanted him to punish me with his.

I couldn't deny my attraction to Riley, but I also wanted to remember what he felt like, intimately. Images filled my brain of what felt like a far away memory... His lips ravaging my own, his tongue wrapped around my cock, him telling me...

I want you.

The words reverberated in my brain as hazy memory tried to surge forth. Of hands and heat, of hard cocks, and those three, little words spoken drunkenly, without thought or consequence. Spoken in truth.

I want you.

I wanted Riley Evans, but I knew I needed to tell him the truth.

I couldn't lie to him anymore. I wanted him to want *me* for me.

Not the me that everyone else got—*XxPrinceAyricxX,* the charismatic performer, Eric the eternal bachelor who knew how to have a good time. I wanted Riley to want me for the lost, childish idiot I was who couldn't breathe when he was in the same room.

My heart beat steadily in my chest as I squeezed my knees tight.

This was it, this was the downfall, I could feel it. I'd flown too close to the sun.

"I know you probably won't believe me, but I don't normally do this sort of thing either," I said, feeling on the spot.

Riley squinted his eyes before brushing some hair out of my eyes. The touch was gentle, and I hated how much I liked it.

I'd been in plenty of scenarios the morning after, both being the one to leave, and the one being left, and usually that was the end of things where I was concerned. But as I stared at Riley in that hotel bedroom, a part of me didn't want this to end.

A part of me wanted to believe that in the mistakes I had made, I could salvage a pure truth.

And that truth was that I was falling in love with Professor Riley Evans.

"Why wouldn't I believe you?" he asked curiously.

The words caused a lump to form in my throat.

"Because, Riley, I—"

But they'd never be spoken. They were lost the moment Riley swiftly caressed my jaw and planted the softest kiss I'd ever felt on my lips.

Riley kissed me like I meant something. Like I was truly *everything* to him, just the way I was.

And God forbid, I wanted to drown in that kiss.

I always dreamed a man would kiss me like that, but no one ever did. Not until that moment.

I kissed him back, not wanting the moment to end.

The vibrant spark between us.

"Shhh... it's okay," he whispered against my lips, brushing his thumb across my jaw.

"Riley..." I whined. Like a total bitch.

Riley's bitch.

Riley pulled me closer, and I fell into him like rain falls to the ground.

The impact, the feel of his warm, smooth chest against my own, his fingers in my hair... It all made me feel lightheaded.

I parted my lips, and he didn't miss a beat as we both fell back against the bed, my cock brushing against the damp, white towel separating us.

Riley slid his tongue in my mouth as his lips traveled over my jaw, down my neck, causing fresh fire to bloom in my blood. My head was pounding, my cock aching as his fingertips grazed my skin.

"Tell me..." he breathed as he draped his hand across my hip.

I allowed my hands to travel over his chest, down his abdomen, resting on the knot where he'd tied the towel closed, absentmindedly brushing my thumb over the bunched fabric.

Riley looked at me and in his eyes I could see he was scared too, though what he had to be scared of was beyond me.

"Tell me to stop," he whispered, letting his forehead fall gently to rest against mine. "Every time I'm near you, all I want to do is touch you..." he breathed, his voice thick with emotion and lust.

And something else I didn't dare acknowledge because I knew I would be doomed, if I did.

"And I know that makes me sound like a total creeper, but—"

I kissed him in return, my own demons clawing at me.

I knew I should have told him to stop. I should have ended things right there, and walked away.

But when Riley Evans kissed me, when he touched me... it felt like everything was perfect for once.

He made me *happy*.

And I didn't want that feeling to go away, so I said, "I don't want you to stop."

Riley kissed me wistfully, rolling me over so that I was on my back, my cock standing up straight with his own admission of excitement a tenting of the white of the towel.

As Riley leaned over me, his towel shifted, revealing his hip lines. The light of morning lit him up like a halo, as he pressed himself against me.

"I never want you to stop," I breathed desperately, imploring his gaze with mine.

Alarm bells sounded off all throughout my body, my brain.

Danger, Eric!

But I'd never felt so strongly about anyone in my life, and so I didn't know how to do anything else at the moment, except be the man Riley Evans wanted.

The man he wanted to kiss, to touch.

I wanted to be *his*.

Riley kissed me once more as he settled his fingers in my hair.

I slid my hands down his sides resting them on his hips.

The towel bunched in my grasp, and within seconds, I felt his hand covering mine.

"Tell me what you want," he purred, his voice full of tenderness as he slid his other hand down my chest. My cock throbbed as I arched my back off the bed, needing to feel his skin on mine.

My head was still pounding, pain mixing with pleasure.

Riley traced his fingertips lightly along my shaft, his touch electric as he mapped each swollen vein.

"Is this what you want?" he asked sweetly, running them up and down my dick.

I found it hard to focus, to breathe, due to the overwhelming feelings culminating in me. His lips pressed against my neck, right over my throbbing pulse, his tongue on my skin felt sweet and warm.

The moan that escaped me was unavoidable.

I wrapped my arms around him, seeking grounding as I pulled him closer. I thrust my engorged cock against his touch, needing more.

"Yes," I breathed, lost in his warmth.

Riley kissed me, his tongue caressing mine as he wrapped his hand around my cock, his palm warm and soft like velvet.

"Is this what *Daddy* wants?" he purred, his lips turning into a smile against mine as he slowly pumped me, brushing his thumb over my slit and through my sticky precum.

God, yes. I want this.

I want him... this man who makes me unable to think or see straight.

This man who drives me crazy.

"Yes," I cried out as my hands settled on his hips once more, which I noticed were now bare. I opened my eyes for a moment to see him above me, naked, his thick, beautiful cock also weeping with delight.

I let my hand slide lazily over his hip, cupping his ass as I looked up into his eyes.

Riley touched me with a reverence I'd never known. Like he truly felt my body was a *gift*.

Like nothing mattered but *this*.

Us.

Riley smirked as he withdrew his hand, sliding down and replacing it with his warm mouth. In one swift motion, he took me into the back of his throat, moaning and groaning as he labored his tongue around my engorged cock.

"Fuck..." I hissed as I fought against his hold. The desire to flip him and be on top, with my cock shoved down his throat was a natural reaction. I didn't like to be *anyone's* bottom.

Riley traced his fingers along my thighs until his hands were beneath my ass cheeks and he was gently lifting me off the bed. The edge of his thumb brushed against my entrance, teasing me, taunting me, and in his grip I was putty.

Resistance was futile, and the second he pressed the edge of his finger against my sensitive entrance, I cried out his name like a prayer.

And in some ways, perhaps that's what Riley was to me.

A prayer, a wish.

A chance to live happily ever after.

When my faculties returned, I turned to him, reaching for his cock.

Riley only smiled, shaking his head. "That's not necessary," he said softly, and he climbed off the bed.

Panic laced through me once again, that I'd done something wrong. Though Riley turned to look at me as he picked up his clothes, his gaze soft and inviting.

"But... I need to take care of you," I whined.

God, the things this man does to me, it's like I don't even know myself!

Riley slid his underwear on, my sight trained on him. He slid his briefs up over his cock, which looked to be softening.

"You already did," he said with a blush. "I'm, uh, going to find some breakfast," he said as he pulled on his shirt.

I watched him like a black and white

movie; intently and with bated breath.

A part of me knew he wouldn't *leave* me, but anxiety and memory told me I'd been in this scenario too many times before to believe it would be different.

"Okay," I said shakily, watching him leave.

I hoped I was wrong.

CHAPTER TWENTY-TWO

Riley

THE RIDE BACK home was much quieter, probably due to the fact we were both more than spent.

Figuratively and physically.

I had meant what I said to Eric. I couldn't remember the last time I had gotten so drunk, or the last time I'd really let my walls down.

Which was most likely thanks to the alcohol.

I knew I should feel ashamed, guilty even, because I'd let myself have a little too much fun, and not only that... the liquid courage was more than to thank for my bold pursuance. For bringing Eric to bed.

But somehow, even though I knew I should be bothered by such things, I wasn't. In fact, I felt like we had turned a corner of sorts.

I had turned a corner of sorts.

For the first time in my life, I felt well and truly free. Like the sky was the limit.

Eric sipped his coffee as we pulled into his driveway, turning the car off. I immediately climbed out, going around to open his door before he could. Seeing the smirk on his face every time gave me a sense of satisfaction. I got the feeling it was hard for Eric to let someone else do things for him, probably because whatever it was he did—which we still hadn't confirmed he wasn't some mafia kingpin, though it was highly unlikely— he was probably the guy in charge, calling the shots. Which only made me like him more.

Just the very thought of him *commanding* me, like he had in our inebriated haze...

Fuck.

My cock stiffened as the memories tried to push forth, but I didn't want to walk down memory lane right now, no matter how nice it was.

I walked him leisurely up his sidewalk, the sun shining brighter than I'd ever noticed before. Eric's shoulders rose and then sunk as he slid his keys out of his pocket, as if he'd let out a huge sigh, though I didn't hear anything. He stood quietly, his lips pursed.

If I didn't know any better, I'd think something was wrong, or perhaps maybe I did something to sour his mood, but I knew from the way I felt—hungover and every bit my age—that he was likely feeling just as under the weather.

His gaze shot up to me, his voice tired. "Thanks for the breakfast, and the ride," he said firmly, though his tone seemed a bit off.

I wasn't too worried, though. Maybe like me, he just needed a couple Advil and a Netflix marathon.

I watched as he turned to open his door, and I couldn't help myself as I stopped him, setting my hand on his wrist.

"Are you busy later? Maybe we could hang out? Grab some dinner, or—"

Eric's shoulders rose and sunk once

more, and he dropped his hand, his bright blue eyes looking almost glassy.

"I... I can't. I, uh, have plans this evening."

"Oh," I said, not at all hiding the disappointment in my voice.

"Yeah, I'm sorry, it's just... I have a lot to do on Saturdays, usually," he said, looking away.

"Catching up on stuff after the work week?" I said, sliding my hands in my pockets as I gave him a soft smile.

"Something like that," he said, his eyes searching mine for something I couldn't quite put my finger on.

I took a step forward and he did not move back.

"When can I see you again?" I asked, my voice much huskier than I meant it to be.

Eric looked up at me like a lost puppy, eyes full of hope and wonder.

A part of me knew I was probably coming on too strong, but the rest of me didn't care.

In Eric's presence, I was bold, and unapologetic, and it felt *good* to be honest, to put myself out there.

"Tomorrow," he said, swallowing

hurriedly. "I can meet you tomorrow, at the cafe?" His voice was somewhat soft, barely a whisper.

I smiled with a nod. "That sounds great," I said.

"Okay then, I'll see you tomorrow morning," he said as he turned from me, opening his door.

I waved to him softly with a smile on my face. Though a part of me wished he would invite me in, I knew it was probably best that I get home myself and catch up on things. Starting with getting out of these tight ass pants and getting into my sweats and recuperating from my night out on the town.

But stupidly enough, the entire way home, I couldn't stop smiling.

Because I felt like for the first time, I was on cloud nine, and I realized that I didn't just *like* Eric and his sexy smirk, I didn't just want to hang out with him.

I was falling in love with him.

Suddenly, I was looking forward to my time off. Looking forward to spending time with him, just letting my guard down and having fun.

Not to mention I can barely keep my hands off of him, and who could blame me?

The man is like the literal embodiment of sex appeal.

He was perfect, and I knew at that moment, I'd made my decision. Tomorrow, at the cafe, I'd gather my bravery and be honest. I'd tell him how I felt. Because I didn't want to lie or hide my true feelings anymore.

I wanted to be with Eric, and the first step was admitting the truth to him. I hoped he would reciprocate. I hoped he'd say yes, to being mine.

My boyfriend.

When I finally made it into my house, exhaustion hit. I pulled off my clothes, seeking the comfort of my lounge wear and the soft cushions of my couch, and I slept.

I slept better than I'd slept in a long time, and I knew it was because for the first time, I was *happy*. Nothing was going to ruin that

CHAPTER TWENTY-THREE

Riley

AFTER A GOOD long nap and a day spent actually relaxing, I felt better than I had in a while. My hangover was even dissipating.

I settled in on my couch with my computer around eight, the first time I'd really gone online all day.

Opening up my laptop, my first task was always checking my email, which was always packed not just with spam and promotional sign ups, but my students were also free to email me if they had questions, or if someone wanted to come in on Sunday afternoon during my set times and use the studio.

I'd gotten through most of my emails when I came across one that was sent from an anonymous address, with the subject "Your boyfriend."

I immediately dismissed it, thinking it was spam or some porn bot initially, but then reality hit me.

My email was my *school email.* That email was filtered pretty good, and I'd never gotten anything remotely sexual on there.

Which only intrigued me more to click open.

There was nothing, but a link. No hello, no sincerely so-and-so, just a link to an Only Fans page.

The email itself was encrypted, and as far as I could tell there was no way to figure out who'd sent it.

Curiosity got the better of me, but I wished it hadn't at that moment. Because that was the moment everything changed.

I clicked the link.

Which brought me to an Only Fans page that was streaming live, and my blood ran straight to my cock as shame, guilt, and panic flooded me.

Eric's bright, beautiful blue eyes stared at me through the screen, his thick, swollen pink cock head sliding through his wet hands. He was naked, on his *bed*, stroking himself as he gazed into the camera, his deep, breathy voice cursing as he slathered his cock in precum, slowly thrusting himself into his hand.

My cock twitched as my blood rushed, my insides turning with arousal as much as panic.

Comments came flying in across the screen, talking about his *daily loads*, saying dirty things I'd only heard in my audiobooks.

I shut the lid of my computer, sucking in a deep breath.

My cock was as solid as marble, and I swallowed harshly as it twitched in my sweatpants.

"What the fuck?" I asked aloud to the empty room, panic lacing through me.

A part of me couldn't believe what I'd seen, thinking I must have imagined it.

My breathing hitched as my cock *throbbed* with need.

Catching my breath, I slowly opened the laptop once more, needing to know if

I had indeed imagined it, or someone was playing a dumb prank on me or something.

The video picked up right where it left off, and sure enough, my eyes did not deceive me.

I watched Eric, or as a cursory glance down at his handle read, *XxPrinceAyricxX, smack* his cock before spitting on it. The memory of his hardness in my mouth only made the strain against my sweats more restrictive, and one glance at the wet spot forming made me feel guilty as all hell, but I knew what I needed to do to feel sane.

So that I could think clearly.

I settled the laptop down on my coffee table before shimmying out of my sweats. My cock sprang free, stiff as a steel pole. My cock head was already pretty wet from the friction of my pants, pressing against a fabric prison. Shakily, I cupped my head, my eyes closing for a brief moment as Eric's breathy moans filled the air.

"You want to watch me fuck my hand?" he purred, his voice through the speakers silky and smooth. It was almost like he was truly in the room with me.

I could hear the comments rolling in, like wind chimes.

"You want to watch me fuck my toy?" he groaned, and I pretended it was me he was talking to.

"Yes," I breathed out loud in the space of my living room, desperate for relief.

Make me your toy...

I watched as Eric smirked on camera, grabbing himself once more. His fingers slid through the sticky mix of precum and spit, and my own cock ached as I increased my pace.

I watched as Eric took some black, sleek contraption, sliding it over his cock. From the front, I watched it disappear, thrusting in tandem. He turned to his side, the view highlighting his defined muscles, his hips and flexing abs as he thrust himself into the sleek toy, and I couldn't help how my mind wandered guiltily down a path I knew I shouldn't traverse.

Eric's voice screwed up as he cursed, groaning as his thrusts increased.

"Fuck!" he cried out as he pulled out,

his release dripping down the silicone, spraying like a damn fountain as he dropped the toy to the floor, bracing himself against the bed.

"Oh fuck!" I cried out in unison as I came, watching his muscles contract as he continued to pump himself, his breath heavy, eyes shut in ecstasy as his release covered his abs.

"I'm sorry," he said, his voice a breathy whisper.

My own orgasm tortured me as I continued my own climax, filled with relief, but also guilt. I closed my eyes as reality set in, and the sound of the video cut out.

I looked at my cum-covered cock, at the black box on the computer screen, at his name in the lower corner.

XxPrinceAyricxX.

The banner at the top of the page listed a boatload of subscribers and I realized all at once, this was what he did.

Eric was a... what?

A stripper?

A porn star?

A... camboy?

My phone dinged, my gaze fixing on it

like a laser beam.

I reached out to the arm of the couch where it lay, picking it up with shaky breath.

Is 10:00 am okay?

Eric's text stared at me from beneath the lit glass of my phone, calling me like a beacon.

My heart raced as I swallowed harshly, running my clean hand over the screen.

Sure.

I texted him back, feeling like the dirtiest human being on the planet. Knowing what he was doing only moments ago.

That I was *watching* him.

Eric sent back a thumbs up, and I dropped my phone as the sob came.

I breathed out a sigh of exasperation as my eyes filled with tears. My softening cock weeped its last bit of release, and I felt so fucking guilty.

This was a dangerous game I'd fallen into.

Eric was dangerous.

While I couldn't deny my attraction to Eric, I knew progressing further into a relationship *now* would be like walking on a tightrope.

If the wrong person recognized him...

I looked at the tab on my screen for my email, my heart sinking.

Perhaps someone already had.

A tear rolled down my face, because I knew what I needed to do.

But I didn't want to.

I really didn't fucking want to.

Because despite the shock, the guilt of what I'd done, what I'd seen...

Somehow I knew it wasn't *him.* Not really.

The Eric I knew was fun, and carefree, and a bit of a brat at times, and I was in love with him.

But I was scared. Scared of the uncertainty, of worrying about whether or not someone would talk, because they clearly knew.

I didn't want to wind up in the Principal's office or something.

No, I needed to do the right thing before things went too far.

They've already gone too far.

I wiped my tears with a shaky hand as I tucked my limp cock back in my pants, closing the lid to the laptop once and for all.

And when I showered that night, not even the hottest water could wash me clean.

CHAPTER TWENTY-FOUR

Eric

I STARED AT my set up, all the lights and equipment, as I hovered over my laptop, which I'd shut down abruptly.

It was like for the first time, they were foreign to me. Like they belonged to someone else.

Tears threatened the edges of my eyes as I slid to the floor, naked, drawing my knees to my chest.

Shame and guilt bloomed in the pit of my stomach.

I'd done my job. The same as I had the day before that, and the day before that.

What was different?

But I knew as I brushed away one of those burgeoning tears *exactly* what was different.

Because the entire time I performed, I was thinking about *him.* Closing my eyes, remembering *his* touch, *his* kiss, *his* smile. All of it.

I no longer derived pleasure from what I was doing, despite doing it well.

And the reality was, I hadn't really *enjoyed* myself the way I did when I was with Riley, or when I thought about him, in a long time.

I looked around my room, at the closet full of designer clothes, my comfortable 1000 count Egyptian cotton sheets.

I'd built this life for myself, by myself, using little more than my looks and sex appeal, and a part of me had always been proud of that. That I was able to make my dreams come true with a little lube and my big cock.

But that night, I felt my dreams shift. I felt myself emerging from some sort of cum-covered cocoon.

I reached for my phone on the ledge of my desk.

The comments were still pouring in, and each one made my heart ache.

I didn't want to hear strangers telling me how thirsty they were, or how they wished they could fuck me.

I wanted to hear *Riley* commanding me, begging me, whispering sweet nothings in my fucking ear like a lovesick puppy.

I swiped up on my screen, brushing past all the comments and tips, bringing up my messenger.

Reaching out for my lifeline, the one person who I thought could calm my sudden hurricane before I spiraled too far out of control.

My fingers shook as I typed out my text, setting a time for tomorrow.

I knew I was reaching, that it wasn't what I really wanted to talk about.

I wanted to tell him the truth.

My fingers hovered over the keys as I thought about what to say, when his *okay* text came in.

I pursed my lips, staring at the text until another name came across my screen. One that didn't text me very often.

Jordan.

I tapped the notification immediately.

I have a proposition for you. If you're interested.

I twisted my lips. Not that I didn't trust Jordan, but I was not in the mood to be someone's stand in again, not right now.

But before I could answer, he texted me a damn novel.

Sticky and I have decided to start shifting our focus and look at more passive income streams. A friend of mine came to me with the idea of putting together a coaching course, kind of like a How-To on how to make bank on OF, but it wouldn't just be OF. She's looking for people who are good at content creation, and I thought maybe you might be interested in joining us. All the coaches are paid directly by her, so there's no middle man or anything. All you need to do is create your course, and once it starts selling on the platform, you get a percentage of the sales from every customer, and you only need to like... engage with them if they have questions.

I stared at the screen for a moment, trying to process his words.

An OF course?

Like... *teaching* someone?

I had to admit, the idea intrigued me.

Though I was also curious as to what caused my friends to *shift* focus.

Sticky's in? I asked.

Sticky's in. I'm sure he'll still do some posting, but I know he's been getting a little burned out as of late, trying to keep up with the demand of our subs.

I raised my eyebrow. Sticky's sex drive was higher than mine, so if he was considering *taking a break*, I knew it had to be something major.

Passive income *helping* others achieve what I did on my own without help.

I couldn't deny it sounded kind of nice, actually. Being able to spread my knowledge. Knowledge that wasn't necessarily tied to my performance skills. Using my brain for once instead of my cock.

I'll do it.

I didn't think twice, answering him. Moments ago, I had wondered if there was more to this, to what I was doing, and then suddenly I had my answer. A way out.

It was like the universe heard me and said, "Here you fucking go, kid."

The relief that washed over me with those three words was immense.

Cool. I'll send you details later.

With that, I was left, feeling like for the first time, maybe things *would* work out for once.

Maybe my luck was truly changing.

CHAPTER TWENTY-FIVE

Riley

I TOSSED AND turned all night, because I couldn't stop thinking about the inevitable, and soon enough, it was time to head to the cafe.

Whereas in the past week or so I'd become accustomed to the butterflies in my stomach when I knew I was going to meet Eric, there were no butterflies this time.

Only anxiety and sadness.

When I got to the cafe, the place was already pretty busy. I took a seat, watching the customers smiling, laughing. I took in the rich scent of coffee and pastries.

It wasn't all that long ago that I was supposed to meet my blind date here. But I'd been busy, and lost track of time, and I missed my shot. But fate intervened, it seemed, and that night I'd gone to M's Place to grab a drink with my brother and lick my wounds.

And that was the night I met Eric.

Almost as if he could read my mind, he waltzed in the door at that very moment, looking as divine as ever. Dressed in a pair of jeans and a black polo shirt, he looked positively sophisticated. His bright blue eyes sparkled like diamonds, and his dark hair was swept back, the light catching the gleam in his raven locks.

Gorgeous.

My stomach turned in knots as he looked at me, my blood rushing beneath the surface, straight to my cock.

He smirked at me, and then I remembered.

I remembered him staring at me through the computer screen, stroking himself and...

I shifted in my seat, if only to stifle my burgeoning erection, because now was certainly not the time to get all hot and bothered.

"Hey," he said as I rose, intending to head to the counter to order a drink.

I needed something to hold, to ground myself to, otherwise I would have sunk right through the floor.

"Hey," I said. I glanced at him as he leaned in toward me.

My heart raced, because I wanted nothing more than to give in and lean into him.

To kiss him like he had tried to kiss me.

But instead, I evaded him, making a beeline for the counter, and ordering a pumpkin spice latte immediately.

Eric didn't seem too bothered by my actions, instead just shrugging and he ordered himself a flat white latte.

When we'd placed our orders and had our drinks—which Eric *insisted* he purchase for us, much to my disdain—there was no turning back.

"Something on your mind, Cinderella?" he drawled, and took a sip of his coffee.

"I just..." I said as I watched the muscles in his forearm tense and flex as he did so, and it only reminded me of the previous night, watching all of his muscles flex as he came.

Beautifully, I might add, but still.

I licked my lips, glancing away from him and sipping my own drink.

How the hell am I going to get through this?

I knew what I wanted to say, and a part of me figured I should just get out with it.

I saw you online, XxPrinceAyricxX.

I know what you do.

I think it might be in our best interest if we just...

But for some reason when I looked at him, that's not what I said. Instead, I said, "It's just this wedding, I guess. We're close to the big day and things are just getting more stressful."

Eric reached out, setting his hand over top of mine. Instinctively, I wanted to pull back, but found it difficult to do so. Like my hand itself was made of iron.

I looked down to where he touched me, running his thumb along my knuckles.

"I mean, I get it. Weddings are a giant pain in the ass."

I scoffed at his remark. "Weddings are a time of love and joy," I said.

Eric let out a dark chuckle. "For some, sure."

"It's just... there are so many details. Things to get absolutely right," I grumbled.

"Isn't that like, the maid of honor's job or something?" Eric asked, raising a brow.

I pulled my hand back, all too aware that his touch was giving me goosebumps and causing my cock to twitch.

"Not everyone has a maid of honor, you know." I wrinkled my nose.

"I'm assuming the bride—"

"Giselle," I corrected.

"I'm assuming Giselle has, like, a ton of bridesmaids. I'm sure they have all the important shit taken care of. All you have to do is hold the rings, plan the party, and look pretty in a suit."

I pursed my lips as I sipped my coffee. This conversation was leaning farther away from what I wished.

Or perhaps, it wasn't, if I was being truthful.

Perhaps I was not the confidant, bold

man I thought I was. Perhaps I was a coward who could not look this man in the eye and tell him, *I know.*

"You would know something about that, wouldn't you? Standing there, looking *pretty,* as you say?" I bit out, watching Eric's eyebrows furrow.

He left his hand on the table, leaning back in his chair languidly. The motion drew my attention to his groin, knowing full well in detail what he was packing beneath his tight, form-fitting pants.

But so did thousands of others.

Call it jealousy, call it petulance.

But I wished it was all for me and no one else, and that made my stomach flip once more.

"I know a thing or two about weddings, actually. I've been a groomsman, like, three times."

I blinked. "You never said..."

Eric shrugged. "You never asked."

Images flipped through my brain of Eric looking pretty in a suit, of him and my brother and party members tossing back shots and dancing with strippers... To that of him wrestling his thick cock out of his suit pants, looking down at me like he looked at me through the computer screen, taunting me to take him into the back of my throat. My own cock twitched in response as my heart lifted, and I nearly jumped when my phone rang.

I didn't even have to look at the name to know who it was, since my brother had his own ringtone, after all.

"Excuse me a second, Eric," I said as I rose from my seat and headed outside, out of earshot.

"Hey, what's up?" I answered, trying to sound normal. The cool air outside the shop was like a balm to my flushed self, and I let out a small sigh of relief.

What sounded like a *sob* on the other end had me on high alert.

My brother *never* cried. Over anything, so the immediate sound was like a giant red flag.

"Aaron, what's wrong, are you okay? Do you need me to come get—"

"It's Giselle," he breathed, his voice heavy.

"Is Giselle okay?" I asked, panicking right along with him.

Giselle was his *world*. She had been ever since they met in college, and I knew then the day he brought her home for Christmas break, there was no denying that one day they'd be the *it* couple of Jasper Springs.

A part of me was jealous, to hear him fall apart over her. I wished someone could love me like that.

With such intensity and depth, the world would stop for them when I walked into a room.

"She's fine, she's..." Another sob, and now I really was worried.

"What, Aaron, she's what?"

"Pregnant, Riley. Giselle is pregnant."

All the blood in my body chilled at those words, warmed only by the remaining ones, full of shock, awe, and happiness.

"I'm going to be a father, Riley. You're going to be an uncle."

I couldn't speak. I could barely process the words as he said them. Giselle was pregnant... and the wedding was only a few weeks away.

"We're not telling anyone, for... obvious reasons," he said, sniffling on the other end.

"Oh," I said, like an idiot, at a loss for words. I wanted to congratulate him, but suddenly the world seemed so vast, I could barely breathe.

I always figured they'd be all in on starting a family, but not this soon.

But I guess, some things don't come on schedule. Including babies.

I turned to look through the window, noticing Eric sitting there nonchalantly, browsing his phone.

For some reason, looking at him snapped me out of my daze, bringing me back to reality.

"Congratulations," I mustered, coming back to Earth.

"Thanks, I just... I needed to talk to someone, sincc, you know, this is kind of a big deal."

"I get it. Can't tell anyone, but you want to tell the world," I said, watching Eric mindlessly sip his latte, waiting for me to return.

To return and break his heart.

Was I capable of that?

Did I want that?

I wasn't so sure, as the very *thought* of not seeing Eric again made my heart palpitate.

"How... how do you feel about the news?" I asked, trying to focus on the subject. I tore my gaze away from Eric.

"I mean, marriage, kids, it's what I always wanted," Aaron said calmly.

"You say that like you're not sure," I spoke cautiously. If my brother was having second thoughts about the news, about the wedding...

"I mean, relationships aren't ever *easy,* you know. You just... when you love someone, you endure whatever you have to, because you know in the long run they're worth it."

I closed my eyes, feeling overwhelmed by the emotion in his voice.

"How do you know?" I asked quietly. "That they're worth it? The pain, the drama, the bullshit. How do you know that it's all going to work out?"

My brother sighed. "I don't. But I know I love Giselle, and I can't imagine my life without her. I can't imagine who I'd be without her, you know? And now..."

I listened as my brother got choked up, talking about his soon to be wife. The love in his voice was evident.

"God, if you would have told us when we were two college kids at a frat party that one day we'd be married with kids, I wouldn't have believed you. But now, all

I can think about is seeing her face at that altar and wondering if this kid will have her eyes," he said, letting out a chuckle. "Our kid is going to be at our wedding, and no one is going to have any fucking clue."

I laughed with him, understanding the levity of this secret. Especially around our mother, who was notorious for sniffing out gossip.

With practically the entire town coming, it was really wild to think about.

I turned to look at Eric once more, catching his gaze. He waved, and I couldn't help but do the same.

"Anyway, I got to go, I just... Thanks, man. Thanks for being you. And listening."

"Your secret is safe with me," I said, and the line went dead.

And as I looked at Eric in the light of the coffee shop, I wondered just how much my still-beating heart could endure.

CHAPTER TWENTY-SIX

Eric

I WATCHED AS Riley came back inside the cafe, dressed in his white shirt and khaki's like some knight in Ralph Lauren.

Thankfully, his brief departure had given me much to think about, and I realized I couldn't do it. I couldn't tell him the truth, until I'd put it behind me.

I wanted to be respectable. I wanted to be *clean* for him.

Sunday Best, and all.

And I couldn't very well go diving headfirst into a relationship with Riley, no matter how bad I wanted it, without cleaning out my closet first.

I needed to go home, make my announcement, and then I could process my next steps.

The road to salvation wasn't going to be easy, but as Riley sat down, crossing his legs in front of me, I knew.

I knew that I was standing on the precipice of a new phase of life. The next phase of my life.

I'd been a groomsman, and I did know a thing or two about weddings, but I'd never considered the possibility of getting married myself. I'd only ever wanted a boyfriend, someone who I could be myself with, my *true* self.

Camming wasn't who I really was. *XxPrinceAyricxX* was someone I had become through guilt and loneliness, and because of that, others responded to him. Because perhaps, they were guilty and lonely too, and I could never begrudge them for that. After all, they made me who I was today.

I only hoped that they would understand that I was ready to move on.

I *needed* to move on.

"Hey, I, uh, I know I just got here but, uh, I have to head out. I have some stuff to take care of. Can we reconvene? Another day?" I asked, both nervous as all hell but also feeling a sense of disappointment.

How had things become so complicated?"

"Yeah, uh, that's probably a good idea. That was my brother, so I, uh, need to get going too."

"Okay, yeah. Cool. That works then. We'll be in touch?" I asked, hopeful.

"Of course," Riley said, smiling. But behind his smile I could tell something was bothering him, but I didn't want to press. Maybe it really was just stupid wedding drama. Been there, done that.

And with that, we parted ways. I climbed into my car and drove home. Walking through the door, I felt a sense of dread as well as relief. I knew what I needed to do.

CHAPTER TWENTY-SEVEN

Eric

I SAT ON my bed, clothed. The lights around me were like a halo, and there wasn't a toy in sight. I didn't want anyone to get the wrong idea. Although my body was used to this, and as such looking at the camera made my cock twitch, I let it be.

Not now, not for everyone else.

I watched the timer as it ticked, the seconds like an eternity.

When I was live, I could see over a hundred people logging on, and I blew out a breath.

This was it.

I looked into the camera and I told them, my long-standing subscribers that there would be no more Daily Load. There would be no more *XxPrinceAyricxX*. I thanked them for their patronage, for their loyalty. For their praises and their tips, and for making a lonely guy feel a little less lonely for a while.

I told them that the years had been great, but it was time for me to simply move on and expand my talents elsewhere.

I told them that I'd met someone, and I wanted to really give it a shot.

The words as I said them were cathartic, and even though I knew I was talking to thousands of people, it didn't feel like I was talking to anyone but myself.

Saying it out loud was the hardest thing I'd ever done.

But the outpouring of *support* from my dirty talkers, my top tier and my bottom tier subs alike, was overwhelming.

Telling me like an old boss how much they'd miss me, but wishing me all the best. Joking at how they would have to find another cock to fantasize over, and praising me that whatever person—because I'd never disclosed my sexuality on my account openly—had my attention was the luckiest person on earth. Especially given what they knew about me, of course.

And when the live ended, I felt relieved. I watched as my account updated, until it disappeared.

It was gone.

Several years worth of content, of comments, of memories. In the flash of a second, it was all gone.

There was no more *XxPrinceAyricxX*.

There was only me.

I breathed out a heavy sigh and tears prickled the edges of my eyes. The lights still shone on me, but there was no audience. There was no performance.

There was just me, my stiff cock, and my bed, for the first time in a long time.

I wiped my tears away as I thought about the levity of such a reality.

I palmed my cock through my pants, feeling a sense of guilt, but also a sense of freedom.

I slowly unzipped my pants, taking my time.

Shimmying out of them felt foreign, despite the fact I'd done it daily for years.

I didn't take my shirt off, or my socks, because I didn't feel like it.

Instead, I leaned back on my bed, my left arm behind my head, using my right to palm my cock slowly. Brushing my thumb over my slit, I relished in the shiver that went up my spine.

I'd been focused on the art of the cumshot for so long, the motions so familiar and repeated, I hadn't truly engaged myself.

It's a strange sort of realization, to come to terms with the fact I *liked* my own touch. That I hadn't really given in to pleasing myself the way I wanted to, even though I thought I had.

My eyes fell closed as my hips bucked of their own accord.

My cock throbbed in my hand as I squeezed it lightly, the sensation causing a moan to escape my throat. Thick and swollen, I removed my hand from behind my head, letting my fingers travel down my abdomen to my base. I squeezed my balls with a light pressure that felt amazing, and my head pebbled with wetness.

I thought about Riley, and his perfect, silken lips wrapped around my cock. I thought about his tongue in my mouth, and his breath on my skin, and I thought about what he would feel like, the weight of him on top of me, pinning me down to the mattress, sliding his thickness inside of me.

My legs stiffened as my core muscles tensed, my veiny cock throbbing with release. I arched my back, my toes curling as my legs stiffened and I writhed in my bed, my hand pushing my cock toward my chest as I came with full force on my shirt.

The relief was euphoric as I lay there in my bed, lazily stroking myself until I'd emptied myself completely, my shirt a sticky mess, my body flushed, and my heart full.

I didn't feel guilty about fantasizing about the man of my fucking dreams, and I didn't feel embarrassed or self conscious about my facial expressions or the way my toes curled or my body twitched when I naturally came.

I felt better than I had in a long time.

I vaguely remembered the phone

going off with notifications as I drifted to sleep, peacefully.

And I dreamed of weddings and cafes, and pretty boys in suits who made me feel whole.

CHAPTER TWENTY-EIGHT

Riley

"WELL?" CHRIS'S VOICE penetrated my thoughts as I realized I'd read the same line in my syllabus three times.

I blinked, turning to face my coworker and friend, as memory dawned on me.

"What's the verdict, Evans? Did you get the ass or not?" he taunted as he took a seat on my counter top. Though it was lunchtime, there were still kids around, and a part of me didn't care if they heard Chris's foul mouth.

I supposed it wasn't the worst thing they could hear.

I didn't really *want* to do the song and dance with Chris. Especially given everything that had happened over the weekend.

But a sliver of me looked at the towering, sporty man who I considered the closest thing I had to a best friend, and I couldn't help myself.

"Please, please, tell me you got laid."

I nodded. "And then some. But..." I sighed, knowing it was best just to purge it all. Get it out in the open so I could grieve the perfection of *Prince Eric.*

Or however he spelled it.

"But?" Chris pressed.

"It's not the mafia. Or a drug dealer," I said calmly.

Chris raised an eyebrow. "Oh? Then what? Stripper?"

"Close. Only Fans. Cam Boy."

Chris's jaw was agape with my admission, a low whistle soon following. He didn't miss a beat. "And you're worried Mr. Only Fans might be bad for your reputation?"

My silence spoke volumes.

"You like this guy, don't you?" Chris's words were serious, all humor dissolved from his tone.

My own admission was harrowing, as I spoke it without thinking.

"I think I'm in love with him."

Chris offered me a soft smile.

"I'm not going to tell you it's not a dangerous game. I'm sure you already know that," he said.

I sighed. "He doesn't know I know. I found out by accident."

"Browsing on your own?" Chris quietly asked.

"Sort of. Anonymous link in my email."

Chris raised his eyebrows in alarm. "Your school email?" he asked.

I nodded. "I tried to look into the sender, but it was encrypted. Believe me, I tried."

"Someone must've seen you two together," Chris said, stroking his chin.

I let out a deep sigh as reality hit me.

Of course, why didn't I think of that.

It could have been a colleague, while we were out partying, but I had a feeling it wasn't. I had a feeling, as I looked at the seat where Trevor Kleypas sat, exactly who'd dropped the bombshell.

He recognized Eric.

And was worried I was making a

mistake.

I wasn't sure whether to be disgusted that he recognized Eric—because I knew what that meant, despite the fact Trevor was one of the early eighteen year old students, so he was technically of legal age to view such content—or to feel a sense of gratitude that he felt strongly enough to look out for me, his teacher. His quiet, shy, *gay* teacher who was apparently out of touch with the dating world.

And all at once, I realized that I had felt the same way. Worried, concerned, that I was perhaps making a mistake.

But as I sat there in my office, talking to Chris, remembering what my brother had said, I knew that was one of those do or die moments.

If I cut things off with Eric for good, would I regret never *enduring*?

Would I always wonder what could have been, if I had put myself first, above my job?

"Yeah, maybe," I said, and Chris smirked.

"Sometimes, in football, there are really hard calls to make. Ones that you know will benefit the team, but might not benefit certain players individually," he said seriously. "Sometimes the risk pays off. And sometimes it doesn't."

I looked at him with my own seriousness and intensity.

"What play do you think I should make, coach?" I asked.

Chris dropped from the counter, standing tall as he slid his hands in his pants pockets.

"I can't tell you that, Evans. That's up to you. But I can tell you that you miss a hundred percent of the shots you don't take."

"Are you quoting The Office to me?" I asked, flashing him with a smile.

"Michael Scott had to get it from somewhere." He winked as the bell rang.

"Thanks, Chris," I said, feeling a little bit better.

"Mhmm," he said as he tapped the top of my glass like it was a basketball hoop, once more.

My brother, Chris... they were both right.

Eric was worth it.

We were worth it, weren't we?

CHAPTER TWENTY-NINE

Eric

"YOU WHAT?" JULIE gasped on the other end of the phone.

"You heard me," I said, tinkering with the cables in my studio as I unhooked my equipment.

Finally, the AC had been fixed, and with my sudden departure from my long-time job, I didn't think I needed *everything* anymore. Just keeping a ring light and a professional mic would be enough for recording my content now.

Jordan had introduced me via email to the founder of Only4U, a platform which housed more than just Jordan,

Sticky, and I, and covered more than just Only Fans.

The owner, Paris, had intentions of launching her platform with courses that covered content creation on all platforms, including TikTok, Instagram, and more. Courses were curated and taught by those who were bigger names on their prospective platforms. Jordan, Sticky, and I were a team, our course content specifically geared toward creating different types of marketable OF content and how to get your content shown and in regular rotation with the algos—even if your content wasn't sex.

Most people tended to think of Only Fans as being a sort of porn hub, and while they wouldn't be incorrect, plenty of people have a variety of non-sexual accounts and content on there—and while sex may have been what we sold for a long time, I didn't start out that way, and neither had the boys.

"How do you feel about this transition?" she asked, surprise still evident in her voice.

"Good, I guess. I mean, maybe a change of pace is good for me. I'm not going to be young forever," I lamented.

"Guess I really do work in social media now," I said with a chuckle.

Julie snickered. "Please, like there aren't thirty-something or fifty-something dudes out there making steamy *Daddy* content."

"And you would know this how, Jules?" I teased.

She snickered on the other end of the phone. "I might be taken, but I ain't dead, Eric."

I laughed a deep, rib-splitting laugh at her words. Julie was truly something else, and a part of me was glad to have a friend like her in my life.

Always supportive, and always a fucking hoot.

Then her tone shifted, changing like the chameleon she truly was.

"So what are you going to do now? About Riley?"

I nearly bumped my head on the desk at her words. I sat back on the floor, tangled in cords.

"I don't know, I haven't uh, really thought about it."

"You should tell him how you feel. Tell him the truth."

I sighed. "The truth is what I've been

dying to tell him since I met him."

"What happened? Why didn't you?"

"Because I worried he'd just split, like everyone else. Because maybe I couldn't face the truth myself."

The silence was palpable between us as I listened to the sound of her soft breaths.

"You deserve to be happy, you know," she said seriously.

"I know, Jules. I just—" I swallowed harshly as I looked at my studio in disarray. "I think I'm on my way there, I just need to take care of some things first, you know."

"I know. I get it. But there's never going to be a right time, Eric. All you have is the here and now, so if you want him... go fucking get him. Tell him the truth, and if he can't see that you are an amazing person, beneath the sex appeal, he isn't for you."

I sighed at the weight of her words. "Do you think he is? For me, I mean."

"Shit, Eric I wouldn't have set you two up for a blind date if I thought you were bad for one another, you know that right? I mean, I like drama as much as the next girl, but I don't need to create any between my friends."

I smirked as I nodded in understanding. "You really think we're good for each other?" I asked, my voice small.

"I know you are. I think you know it too."

Just at that moment, Riley texted me. I swiped up, telling Julie I had to go, and she didn't press me.

Instead, she told me good luck, and hung up as I stared at Riley's text.

How about a do-over? Tomorrow night is bar bingo at M's Place...

I didn't hesitate to answer, *Yes, it's a date.*

CHAPTER THIRTY

Eric

M'S PLACE WAS always packed on Bar Bingo & Karaoke night. We'd agreed to meet up separately only because at the last minute, he had something work related to take care of via his Principal. A part of me was nervous, worried that somehow it had to do with me, or rather who I *was*, but I tried not to get too worked up.

Considering the fact I had shut down my online personal forty-eight hours ago.

Which also was the last time I—

"Hey."

Riley's smooth voice pulled me and my desperate cock from the grandeur of fantasy, and I had to do a double take. He stood in front of me like he had that first night we'd gone to the arcade together. Dressed down in dark jeans and a graphic tee shirt that sported some sort of dragon or something against heathered gray fabric. His light hair looked golden in the light of the bar, and my cock throbbed in time with my heart.

"Well, well, looks like Cinderella finally made it to the ball," I teased.

Riley looked a little worried, a little disheveled, running his hand through his hair. It wasn't a bad look on him, though.

I sipped my rum and coke, motioning for him to take a seat in front of the cards I placed in front of him, along with a bingo dabber.

One of the waitresses came by to take our drink order, or rather Riley's drink order, since I had started early. When she was gone, he looked at me with a slight expression of confusion.

"You got my cards," he mumbled, like some dazed teenager.

"I mean, it *is* bar bingo, and it's a game. You know how I like games. I think you like them too," I said, flashing him with a smirk.

The blush that crept onto his cheeks was my answer.

"I do. Like games, I mean, but... Eric..."

My eyebrows furrowed as his tone turned soft, worried.

"Is something wrong?" I asked, panic striking me.

Riley sighed, sliding his dabber up toward me. He tapped his long fingers on the table, biting his bottom lip before he said, "There's something I need to tell you."

"Actually, there's something I need to tell you too," I said, and took a sip of my drink.

"Really?" he asked, deadpan.

I nodded. "Yeah, but, uh, you first."

CHAPTER THIRTY-ONE

Riley

IT WAS NOW or never.

"I, uh... came across something yesterday," I said, my entire body shaking like a leaf.

Eric's eyebrows furrowed with concern, and I let out a deep breath.

"I saw you. Online, I mean..." I said the words, and the moment they left my mouth I felt relief.

But that relief soon dissipated as I watched Eric's smile falter, as I watched his furrowing brows tighten, and his shoulders sink.

He didn't deny my words, or try to

refute them.

But the sight of his sadness pulled at my heart and all I wanted to do was hug him.

But I was frozen in place, watching him.

"I can explain..." he said softly.

"I don't know if you need to, but..."

"I wanted to tell you, but I didn't know how. I worried that maybe—"

"What?" I asked, my voice faraway as I let myself get lost in his sapphire gaze, his youthful effervescence.

"I was worried you might... you know... want to stop whatever... this is."

"What is this?" I asked curiously, motioning between us. "Because ever since I met you, I haven't been able to define what this is. We're friends, I thought at first, but ever since the weekend, since the hotel, I—"

My words were jumbled in my brain as I tried to make sense of them, as emotion plagued me.

"I have friends. I don't feel a fraction for them, what I feel for you." I looked at him with a mixture of fear and hope.

Would he understand?

That he was worth it?

That despite the obstacles in our path—our jobs—that maybe this was fate?

"Say something," I pleaded, watching him bite his lip. "Say I'm crazy, and we can forget all of it. The games, the sex... Tell me you don't feel anything, and we can just be friends."

Eric's lips twitched at the words, his eyes sparkling with the beginnings of a somber mist.

"I don't want to be friends, Riley. I can't be friends with you," he said firmly.

"Oh," I said, feeling the worst rejection I think I'd ever felt in my life.

"I can't be friends with you when you're all I think about when I'm alone. Just me. I can't be friends with you when every time I'm near you I—"

He let out a deep sigh as my heart threatened to skip a beat.

"I should have told you the truth, about me. About what I *did*, but honestly, my experience in life taught me as soon as I did tell someone what I did, they peaced the fuck out, and I didn't want you to peace the fuck out," he said, twirling his straw in his glass. He looked at the cards, then at me as our waitress dropped off my beer.

"It was selfish, I know that. But when it comes to you I can't help my selfish desire. To be whoever you want me to be. To be wherever you are."

"Eric..." I breathed his name like the prayer it truly was.

"The other night, that was the last straw, just so you know. After I..."

The silence spoke volumes as we both caught one another's gaze, and he sucked in a breath.

"I'd been performing a long time before I met you, and I don't regret doing it for as long as I had. I only regret not ending it sooner, before I—"

"What?" I asked, leaning closer, hanging on his every breath, his every word.

Waiting for the words I dared to hope to hear.

"Before I fell in love with you." He said the words boldly, confidently, and my heart threatened to beat right up out of my chest.

I pushed away from the table, and rose to my feet. The look in his eyes killed me, because I knew he thought I was going to be like the others. I was going to walk away.

And in all reality and truth, I should have.

But I loved him too.

And love... it endures. It fights and it dances, and it wins and it loses.

But it always persists, even in the darkest of hours.

I moved toward him slowly, and he stood of his own accord, ready for an argument or defense, neither of which he'd need.

Because I knew as I looked at him, that he was more than what he displayed to the world.

I took his face in my hands, imploring his gaze with my own. I was well aware of our public display, and I didn't care.

I only wanted to soothe this man's worries, to show him I wasn't going to run.

I wanted to double down on our bets. Play the long game.

"What you do... it's not who you are. I know that better than anyone," I told him, rubbing my thumb along his jaw.

Eric looked up at me with glassy blue eyes. "You do?" he asked, his breath shaky. Vulnerable.

I nodded, letting my thumb brush over his lower lip. "You are a cocky, pain in the ass pretty boy who hates to lose," I said with a grin. "Whose voice is like velvet, and who I can't stop thinking about."

Eric parted his lips as a soft sigh escaped, settling his shaky hand on my hip.

"Besides, you still have yet to beat me at anything," I said with a smirk.

"Is that so?" Eric said, licking his lips.

I nodded. "I believe the score is Eric zero, Riley three."

Eric shook his head, grunting in response. "We'll see about that."

I swiftly tucked my finger under his chin, tilting his head up as I lowered mine, capturing his lips with my own.

Eric did not fight me, nor did he resist my advance.

I steadied him with my left hand as he sank against me, lifeless in my arms, under my ministrations. He parted his lips, and I desperately devoured his kiss, stroking his tongue with mine. My cock twitched, and he let out a small laugh.

"Maybe the score is Eric two , Riley three," he drawled against my lips.

"How so?" I asked as we broke away from each other's maddening kiss.

"Well, I certainly won where your cock is concerned. And perhaps your heart."

I smiled, shaking my head as he took his seat, crossing his legs like the cocky asshole he was.

And I took his bait.

I'd always take his bait, I realized. Because I loved playing with him just as much as he loved to rile me up.

"Yes, well, the night is still young. Perhaps there will be more victories in both of our cards."

Eric grinned wickedly. "Let's sweeten the stakes then. You win bingo, I'll sing like a canary for you and everyone here, whatever song you chose."

I shrugged. "Hmmm... I'm thinking Taylor Swift, or Axe 2 Grind..." I mused, flashing him with a grin of my own.

Eric rolled his eyes. "If I win bingo..." His voice was dark, inviting, and sinfully sweet. "If I win, you have to let me draw you like one of your French girls. And by that, I mean naked," he said with a shrug.

I raised an eyebrow at him. "Really Eric? You want to be the Jack Dawson to my Rose?" I laughed.

"Well, I wasn't sure you'd get the reference *old man*, but surely as a *professor of art*, you are well acquainted with the male form and how it is... inspiring, no?" he said, gleefully attempting a horrid French accent.

But all stereotypes aside, it was kind of funny, and I couldn't help but smile.

"Deal," I said as I took my seat and the MC took the stage to start calling numbers. But as far as I was concerned, I'd already won more than the game.

CHAPTER THIRTY-TWO

Eric

WE STOOD ON my porch, like two awkward teenagers, as I fumbled with my keys.

"Do you want to come in?" I asked, feeling for the first time like I had nothing to hide.

Because we were both on the same page.

"Only if you're comfortable," Riley said sweetly, leaning down to deliver a quick kiss to my lip. "You are the one in charge here, and I am a gentleman, after all," he said, flashing me with a soft smile.

"Then yes," I breathed, not thinking twice. "Yes, I want you to come in."

Riley smiled, nodding as I opened the door for him. He peered inside before taking a step in, and I followed.

My lights came on automatically as I shut the door.

A low whistle escaped his throat.

"Wow..." he said in awe, looking around my open concept living space.

"Wow as in good wow, or—"

Riley turned to face me as I slid my hands in my pockets, leaning against my sectional.

"Did... your job pay for this house?" he asked, though his tone was not judgmental as it was shocked.

I nodded, crossing my arms. "Yes. Took a while, because at first I didn't really know what I was doing, but once I figured out how to market, how to follow the algos, how to create engaging content, both sexual and non-sexual... I was able to finally monetize my content and buy a house. In a nice neighborhood, with nice neighbors, and..."

I realized I was rambling, and he was staring. He beamed at me with *pride.*

And it felt more than good to have someone look at me, the real me, and see the success I'd had, no matter how I'd come across it.

"That's amazing," he said as he stepped toward me and settled his hand on my waist.

"Like a Rubix Cube, so many intricate parts make up who you are," he said, pulling me to him.

I slid my arms around his neck, looking up at him with so much love I could have been the heart eyes emoji.

"I'll never regret the things I did to get here, but I'm excited for this next chapter," I breathed against him.

Riley's eyebrows narrowed. "What's the next chapter?"

"I told you, after the other night, I closed my account. My friends slash coworkers, the guys from the pool game, we're going in as a team on a platform that teaches... well, anyone I guess who wants to know... about content creation and making a six figure business out of whatever it is you're passionate about, I guess."

Riley gleamed with pride. "That sounds amazing."

"Well, it kind of just happened to come at the right time, you know. I was ready to be done with performing because..."

My words disappeared as I looked at him, as I took in the sight of this man who inspired me to be the best version of myself I could be.

"I wanted *only* you," I whispered, pulling him into my kiss. "And I wanted you to be the only one who got me, all of me," I breathed, biting my lip as I let the words out, their finality like glass in the air between us.

Riley settled his hand on my collarbone, forcing me to look up at him as he nodded.

"You aren't the only one with selfish desires, Eric," he breathed as he slid his hands down my shirt to my waistband.

His fingers gently tugged at my belt, swiftly undoing the buckle, and my cock twitched. I looked into his eyes and knew, I'd never want anyone else.

Riley Evans was end game.

I settled my hands on his hips, tugging at the hem of his shirt. He let me remove it without question, and I had to stifle a groan as I laid eyes on his perfectly defined chest, lit up by the amber lighting of my sconces.

"Is that so?" I asked, raising a brow. "Why don't you tell me more about these... selfish desires?" I let my voice go dark and gravelly in the way I had learned most people liked.

Deep, sexy, with a tinge of growl.

Riley responded by shoving my pants and underwear to my ankles. My cock bobbed free, stiff as a board.

Desire was never a problem with Riley in mind.

He pulled me closer, his fingers curling in the hem of my shirt as he kissed my neck, right over my pulsing vein, before he removed my shirt, leaving me completely naked.

"Hmm... well, let's see... For starters..." He kissed my lips, his tongue hungry for mine as he squeezed my cock in his warm palm.

I groaned from the touch as he stroked me. I couldn't help but thrust my hand against him, seeking more, needing more.

More of his touch, more of his love.

More of *him.*

"I want to taste you," he breathed in

my ear.

I was more than happy to oblige, picking up what he was throwing down.

"You want to choke on *Daddy*'s cock, huh? Want to wrap that hot little mouth around me until I come down your throat?" I taunted him.

He responded to my shift in demeanor, just as I knew he would, and I couldn't deny the way that simple shift, the way he just *obeyed* me as he dropped to his knees, eyes imploring mine, made me feel.

Like I truly was the king of this castle, like I was the king of his heart.

And his cock, which visibly strained against his jeans.

He reached for me, but I backed away.

"Ah, ah, I didn't say you could have this yet," I teased, assuming the role that was easiest for me, a role that I had a feeling was just what the professor needed.

Someone to take control of the situation, take control of *him.*

"Please," he said, licking his lips.

"Show Daddy how much you want this cock," I said as I approached him, letting my moistened tip brush the edge of his silky lips.

"Show me that pretty pink cock of yours," I commanded, and Riley did not hesitate. He removed his pants and boxers faster than I could blink.

"Sit on the couch," I ordered, and he did, leaning back against my gray cushions so I could take in the sight of him, all long legs and arms, toned and defined by the shadows the light was casting on him, his thick, pink cock standing at attention.

The last time we'd really gotten intimate, things were a blur. And then the next morning, when we'd gotten carried away, I'd walked away with my needs met, but Riley...

Riley had insisted he was fine, but I never got to reciprocate the pleasure like I'd wanted to.

As badly as I wanted this man's mouth on my cock, I wanted to please him, to make him feel as good as he made me feel.

I straddled his hips as I braced my knees on the cushions, letting my cock brush against his. His arms stretched out like a trapeze along the back of my couch, his dark eyes gazing into mine with warmth and wonder.

"That's a good boy," I purred as I captured his lips with mine, rubbing myself against him. I pulled away for a moment, taking stock of his lustful gaze, smirking as I spit in my hand. His eyes widened.

"Is that what you want, Cinderella?" I asked as I slathered both of our cocks in my saliva.

I could feel the stickiness of precum mixing with the warmth of my spit. I slid my hand over his leaking head, gathering it as I coated myself in it. In *him*.

"Yes," he breathed, his fingernails digging into my ass.

I smirked, commanding him once more. "Then get on your knees, Princess."

Riley didn't waste a moment as he did as I asked, nearly knocking me to the floor as he did so. The moment his mouth wrapped around my cock, I felt like my entire body turned to liquid.

Riley hollowed his cheeks, taking me to the back of his throat in one swift motion.

I grabbed his hair, letting out a deep growl, mixed with cursing as his tongue lapped at my head, pushing into my slit.

I pulled out, if only because I didn't want to come yet, and I knew if Riley kept it up, I wouldn't last long.

I wanted to give him what he wanted, but I also wanted to take my time.

"Not yet, baby," I murmured huskily as he looked up at me, doe-eyed and needy.

"If you recall, I did win bar bingo. I need to collect my prize," I breathed out, trying to catch my breath.

Riley pursed his lips, nodding. "Oh... okay."

"Now, show me that fine ass I have had the pleasure of looking at all night," I commanded.

Riley blushed, but he did as I asked, bracing himself against the arm of my couch, propping out his ass for me like a nude model.

"I did say I wanted to draw you naked," I teased, tracing my fingers up his thighs, over the curve of his ass, in the dip of his back and up his spine.

Then I licked him where I'd touched him, watching as his thighs tightened and he thrust himself against my couch arm with need.

"I just didn't tell you my medium of choice would be my tongue," I whispered in his ear.

His skin was decorated with goosebumps as he shivered.

"Too much?" I asked, placing a kiss on his neck, beneath his silky hair. I could feel his pulse against my tongue, my cock aching for release.

"No, not enough," he breathed, his voice strained.

I slipped my hand beneath him, between the couch and his stomach, pulling him back against my raging cock as I grabbed his.

"We can stop if you want to, if you're not comfortable," I whispered.

Riley looked at me over his shoulder, arching his back as he brushed his ass against my stiffness, causing me to suck in a breath.

"I don't want to stop," he breathed, his eyes full of heat, and something else.

Love.

I smirked as he spread his legs apart, his gaze imploring mine.

"I need to hear you say it," I said,

breaking character for a moment, if only because I was already so close to the edge, I didn't know if I would make it myself.

Riley parted his perfect lips, still swollen from kissing me.

"I want you, Eric." he breathed, my name full of so much love and wonder. "I want you to feel me... and in every thrust, every beat of my heart, I want you to know that it beats for you."

I kissed his shoulder softly, trailing kisses down his spine until I reached his ass. I spit on his hole as I gathered more wetness from his leaking cock in my other hand. In tandem, I worked both with my torturous fingers, taking my time as I slowly pumped his cock with one hand, working my way up to two fingers in his tight entrance. His thighs tightened, and he grit his teeth as I licked the puckered flesh before sliding a third in, and I didn't miss the way his cock twitched in my hand as I did so.

"Are you sure?" I asked, my lips trailing up his spine, assaulting his neck.

Riley nodded vehemently. "Yes," he said, his voice a hoarse whisper. "Make me come, Daddy." His voice was solid, unwavering, and his gaze spellbinding as he looked at me.

I would give this man anything and everything he asked for, now and forever.

I grinned wickedly, capturing his gaze and never dropping it as I quickly slid a condom down my shaft. I watched as his pupils enlarged, as his jaw tensed, as his eyebrows furrowed. I watched his mouth form a tiny 'o' as I breached him, felt his entire body tense.

"Just breathe," I said, though I wasn't sure who I was talking to, myself or him.

Slowly, I fit myself inside him and his body welcomed me like a glove. And for a moment, we stood there, unmoving, connected in the most basic, most primal of ways.

His cock throbbed in my hand as his breath shook.

"I love you," he whispered, his lips planting a soft kiss on mine.

Three words.

Those three words I never thought would bring me such peace, were my undoing.

I thrust my hips slowly against him.

In my mouth, he groaned as I slid myself out, slowly inching in again until we'd both accustomed ourselves to the feel of one another. Slow and steady, we rocked together, my cock in his warm, tight ass and his cock in my warm, tight hand.

It felt like hours, but in reality it was probably mere minutes. When I broke away from his kiss, I buried my face in his hair, unable to hold off any longer. I gritted my release out through my teeth, stilling inside him as he let out his own moan of ecstasy, coating my hand in thick, warm release, until we both collapsed against the couch, spent and sated.

"I love you too," I whispered against his neck, feeling overwhelmed with happiness.

EPILOGUE

Riley

I KNEW THE closer I got to the wedding, the more stressed I'd be. But at least I didn't have to worry about finding a plus one.

"So, what really is there left to do?" Eric asked, sipping on his drink.

"What is there left to do?" Giselle looked like she was about to pop a vein.

"The girls still need to pick up their dresses, the guys need their tuxes, I need to finalize with the caterer..."

"Who's your caterer?" Eric asked as Aaron supportively stroked his wife and mother-to-be's shoulders.

No one had made a comment about Giselle's sudden shift in drinks, which led me to believe they also knew and had been sworn to secrecy, or perhaps they weren't that observant.

"Penn's Bakery..." she said. "Why?"

Eric pointed over to the jukebox. "Like, Penn Barrett?"

Giselle opened her mouth as Eric shrugged. "He's over there, talking to Mitchell. You do know, Mitchell, like, Jasper Springs's fucking paparazzi?"

Giselle let out a deep breath, fixing her expression.

"I do. Mitchell is my photographer, actually."

Eric smiled. "Well, it must be your lucky day, because they're both in some heated discussion over there. Probably should go break it up before hands are thrown," he said with a chuckle.

"Standing over there with the that sexy vet and Weston Rhodes."

Lane laughed as Grayson rolled his eyes.

"You know Weston Rhodes?" Lacey asked, surprised.

"Yeah, he's my neighbor."

The looks from the party were

shocked.

"You live in Jasper Springs Estates?" Henry perked up.

"Yeah, been there since I was like, I don't know, twenty-two."

"What the hell are you? The next Paris Hilton?" Aaron said as Giselle headed over to talk to the boys.

"More like, if I told you I'd have to kill you," Eric said with a wink.

"Ah, the pretty ones are always either gay or criminals, alas." Lacey sighed.

"Or argumentive photographers," Grayson mewled, as everyone else chuckled.

"What's so funny?" Henry asked.

Julie made a sour face as she pushed her Mai Tai toward Eric. "Ugh, this is way too sweet for me, please take this."

Eric shrugged, taking a sip, puckering his lips. "Yeah, that's tart," he said.

"Mitchell is quite an opinionated man," Grayson shrugged. "I don't think there's a soul in Jasper Springs he hasn't pissed off."

"Isn't that, like, bad for a photographer? Don't you want, like, a good reputation?" Henry asked curiously.

"I mean, we don't actually know what happened. All we know is the gossip that gets spread, and in my experience, gossip is only like thirty percent true." Eric chortled.

"True," Julie agreed as we all watched Aaron and Lacey head over to where the boys were standing.

That was the moment the crowd roared with excitement as Jasper Springs's favorite musician rolled into the bar.

"Nice of you to make it, Drew," Julie said as she hugged Taylor and his rockstar beau.

"You know I wouldn't miss this wedding for the world," he teased. "Besides, I'm kinda digging this place," he said, flashing a megawatt smile.

"It does have its charms," Eric said as he raised his glass, and everyone else at the table agreed, raising theirs in response.

"I can't believe we're only one week away," I whined. "Which reminds me..."

Eric looked up from his drink.

"Have you found suitable *attire* for the wedding yet?" I asked, knowing full well the man in question had a closet full of suits.

But I wasn't asking about his daytime attire.

With Eric officially as my plus one—and with the title of *boyfriend*—I too had turned a corner.

While I might have been shy, quiet, and reserved in my day to day life out of preservation, even before I'd met the man, there was a sense of freedom that I was now able to explore parts of myself I'd hidden for far too long.

And with the freedom and support from my boyfriend, I was starting to feel comfortable with myself and my *preferences* in a way I'd never vocalized until now.

Because I'd never been *comfortable* with anyone, the way I was with Eric. He didn't judge me for the literature I'd consumed, or the fantasies I held, and he certainly didn't judge me when I wanted to shut the world out and have some drinks and play some games.

And I'd also learned, that my *Daddy* liked to give up control once in a while himself. Something that was as foreign to him as taking control was to me.

Both of us were learning how to explore the parts of ourselves we'd kept hidden, and there was a contentness in sharing that experience.

Being with Eric was the easiest thing I'd ever done. He fit into my life, into my heart like the glass slipper fit Cinderella.

"I think I've found some *sufficient* accessories, yes," he replied, not missing a beat, smirking devilishly.

"I hope they aren't too uncomfortable," I said, heat filling my cheeks, as I knew what we were talking about was exclusive to us.

Eric twisted his hands together, his fingertips feathering over the skin of his wrists, where he still sported a little rope burn beneath his watch.

"Not at all," he said, his eyes sparkling. "But you will have to wait until the wedding to see my full ensemble," he said, his tone cocky and full of attitude, making my cock twitch once more.

"Some things are worth the wait," I said coolly, brushing him off, knowing all the while it would drive him mad.

And as I sipped my beer, laughing with my friends, my arm around my boyfriend's shoulders, I couldn't help but think the best was yet to come.

Thank you for reading Eric and Riley's story.

If you enjoyed this book, please return to your favorite retailer and leave a review. Even a few words could mean the world to an author.

Continue the series with Mitch's story, Book 6 in Jasper Springs!

OTHER BOOKS BY EVIE

Federal Protection Agency
Mason
Rafe
Ryzen
Cooper
Noah
Damien
Sebastian
Gabe
Logan

Ruthless Empire
Courting Danger
Chasing Danger
Kissing Danger

Smokejumpers
Hawke
Cyrus
Jase
Gage
Jackson
Xavier

Jasper Springs
Cade
Dawson
Drew
Grayson
Riley
Mitch

From The Edge
Shattered
Runaway
Jaded
Rescue
Hidden
Tormented

Gray Vale Pack
His Fated Mate
His Wounded Warrior
His Healing Heart

ABOUT THE AUTHOR

Evie Riley is a prolific, neurodivergent author known for her captivating MM romance novels. She has gained a significant following and topped the LGBT+ action and adventure bestseller charts with her series.

Evie's writing style often explores dark and gritty themes where her men must overcome difficult obstacles in their search for love, but she has also ventured into sweeter small-town romances, incorporating tropes like enemies-to-lovers, friends-to-lovers, age-gap, and forced proximity. She is known for crafting engaging romantic suspense novels and has a knack for creating interconnected series worlds that keep readers invested.

Interestingly, Ms. Riley has hinted at exploring new genres, such as Alien Omegaverse Romance, in the future.

Outside of writing, she enjoys spending time at the beach and has a quirky personality, described by her partner as ranging from cute to deadly, depending on her blood-chocolate levels.

Evie spends her nights writing bad boys in love, and her days wrangling the sweet boys she loves.